THE
GREAT
Ice-Cream
HEIST

Also by Elen Caldecott

How Kirsty Jenkins Stole the Elephant
How Ali Ferguson Saved Houdini
Operation Eiffel Tower
The Mystery of Wickworth Manor

ELEN CALDECOTT

BLOOMSBURY

LONDON   NEW DELHI   NEW YORK   SYDNEY

Bloomsbury Publishing, London, New Delhi, New York and Sydney

First published in Great Britain in June 2013 by Bloomsbury Publishing Plc
50 Bedford Square, London WC1B 3DP

A CIP catalogue record for this book is available from the British Library

ISBN 978 1 4088 2050 6

MIX
Paper from
responsible sources
FSC® C020471

Typeset by Hewer Text UK Ltd, Edinburgh
Printed and bound in Great Britain by CPI Group (UK) Ltd, Croydon CRO 4YY

1 3 5 7 9 10 8 6 4 2

www.bloomsbury.com
www.elencaldecott.com

To Mo and Andrew, with thanks for their help

CHAPTER 1

The boy lay on top of the shed roof with his arms and legs splayed. He wore a T-shirt with a huge face on the front. If Eva scrunched up her eyes, his pale limbs spread against the black background looked like a pirate flag. Though if she unscrunched her eyes, he just looked like a boy hiding from the fighting going on beneath him.

He hadn't spotted her watching him.

From her bedroom window, Eva could see the gardens behind the houses, all joined together. Hers and the boy next door's.

Her own garden was neat and ordered. A shed, a swing, borders that ran around the grass like a picture frame. There was a scuffed brown scab of earth beneath the swing that Dad sighed over.

Next door was different.

It was a hot people soup. She could see five people in shorts and T-shirts sweating on plastic chairs. The space was small, but they crowded in like sardines in sportswear. Dotted around the concrete yard were plants and dogs, all drooping in the heat. Bottles and ashtrays and magazines filled the rest of the space, as though every single centimetre had to be used to make it worth paying the rent.

Two young men were wrestling. The people sitting on the chairs yelled encouragement. It wasn't clear who was winning.

The boy on the shed roof ignored them all.

He was lying starfished in sunshine, his arms and legs spread out to catch the warmth. He lay still, as though the adults were nothing to do with him. As though the other McIntyres weren't his business at all.

The McIntyres had moved in next door about a month ago. They had arrived in a white van and a torrent of noise. Their furniture came in drips and drops all day, the little van driving back and forth, bringing their stuff from wherever they'd lived before.

Eva had watched them. Once or twice Dad had told her to mind her own beeswax, but she hadn't been able to stay away.

New neighbours was the first interesting thing to happen in a long time. And Eva had wanted to know about these new people. There was a mum and a dad and lots of boys. She hadn't been sure which of the boys were staying and which were just helping with the move. There were dogs too, two of them with wide jaws and wider shoulders. She had watched them all. Watched and watched until the street lights came on.

Dad had been quiet, staying at the back of the house, in the kitchen, or out in the garden. When she'd asked why, he'd just scowled and said 'McIntyres', as if that explained everything.

Eva soon learned what he meant.

In the garden below, the two wrestlers spun around hard. One flailed for a second, like a cartoon character trying to stay in mid-air, then he fell heavily against a chair. The woman who had been sitting in it, Mrs McIntyre, spilled to the ground. She leapt up, yelling. Soon, the whole lot were in uproar, blaming each other, laughing, shouting. The party moved indoors and Eva heard the thump of bass as music started. It would probably carry on into the night.

On the shed roof, the boy opened his eyes and grinned.

Eva leapt back.

Had he seen her spying?

CHAPTER 2

Outside, the sky was beginning to turn pink. The thud of bass still came through the wall. Eva's dad threw himself back on to the sofa as though he were falling on to a bouncy castle. The sofa, which was not a bouncy castle, harrumphed in alarm. Or, at least, that's what the noise sounded like to Eva.

'The sofa will leave home if you keep treating it like that,' Eva said.

'Will it?' Dad grinned.

'Yup.' Eva pushed her beanbag even closer to where Dad sat. 'It will pack its suitcase and go. You'll see it getting the number 56 bus into town and that will be that. You'll have to sit on the floor.'

Dad laughed. Eva could always make Dad laugh, even if he was having a sad day.

'Well, I'll try to be nicer to the furniture then. We

don't want to live in an empty house. So, what have you been up to today? Did you have a good time with Jaclyn?'

Jaclyn was Gran. Eva always spent the school holidays with Gran while Dad was at work. Well, always since two years ago. But Eva didn't let that thought get too close; she punched it on the nose before it could properly form. Her day today, that's what Dad had asked about. They had done a grocery shop in the morning, then some dusting and a telly programme about moving abroad. She could do better than that for Dad though.

She tilted her head back to look at him. His eyes were closed and his eyelashes rested on his cheeks like tiny brushes. But he was definitely listening. She could tell by the way a corner of his mouth was tilted up.

'Well,' she said. 'As you know, I was woken by the sound of the town siren calling in all the superheroes. I flew down to police headquarters in time to find a mass jailbreak had the citizens in terror. Luckily, I trapped the escaped convicts in the town hall. Once they were all inside, I used my superpowers to stop time while the police went in to round everyone up.'

Dad was smiling properly now. The lines at the side of his mouth looked like lots of brackets from where Eva was sitting.

'Did you, now?' he said.

Something banged next door, maybe a door being slammed.

Eva let her head drop on to the edge of the sofa. She wished she *had* had a superhero kind of day. Suddenly she felt a bit sad. It happened like that sometimes. She could be in the middle of laughing and making up stories for Dad, and then the blues would come.

Dad seemed to notice her change of mood. She felt his hand come to rest on the back of her head. The last rays of sunlight spilled in through the open blinds and cast shadows like prison bars across the floor.

'What should we do this evening?' Dad asked. 'Game of Boggle? Or maybe a bit of *The Only Book in the World*?'

The Only Book in the World was Dad's joke. It was what he called *The Twits*. She knew it off by heart. Which was why she always read it. Every other book was too hard. The words in them were like barcodes and her scanner was on the blink. *The Twits* was safe.

Eva didn't think it was a funny joke. She drew her legs in and tucked her knees tight to her chest.

'We can play Boggle with two-letter words if you like,' Dad said.

'You'll still win.'

'I'll give you a ten-point head start?'

Eva flipped over on her beanbag so that her face was buried in the beans and her bum stuck up in the air. Doing an ostrich.

'Eva?' Dad laughed.

Even deep in the beanbag she could feel her bottom lip sticking out. Mum used to call it a slug-sulk because it was like having a slug stuck to her face. Mum would tease her about having creepy-crawlies on her chin until Eva laughed and the slug-sulk was gone.

'Like that is it?' Dad asked. 'Don't worry, Ladybug, it was just a thought. How about a takeaway and a bit of telly instead?'

The lip-slug vanished and Eva smiled. That sounded much better.

'Chinese?' she asked.

'Chinese. Should I get the menu, or do you want the usual?'

'The usual.'

Outside, someone shouted and a car squealed away.

Dad slipped his phone from his pocket. 'Your wish is my desire,' he said. His arm stopped in mid-air, the phone held up like an Olympic torch. 'Oh, but we have to wait a bit. Your gran's coming over. She has something she wants to talk about.'

'What?' Eva asked.

'I don't know,' Dad frowned a little. 'She sounded a bit serious on the phone.'

Eva felt a flutter of panic in her chest, like moths beating against a light bulb. Dad must have noticed.

'Don't fret,' he said. 'I'm sure it's nothing to worry about. I'm sure it's nothing at all.'

CHAPTER 3

Eva was in bed, her duvet pulled up to her chin. Her eyes were wide open, though she was meant to be asleep. Her room had blue striped walls and blue striped curtains. Dad said it looked like a giant deckchair. Tonight, with the light off, the stripes were jail grey.

Gran and Dad were downstairs. They had sent her to bed earlier than usual so that they could talk.

If she really were a superhero, she'd be able to hear through walls, or send out a monitoring bug to relay the conversation back.

But she was a normal girl, with normal ears, and she couldn't hear a thing.

At least, not from here.

Eva pushed back the duvet gently and stepped softly towards the door. Dad always left it open a bit to let in light from the landing. She pulled it open, ever so slowly, and then stepped out.

She could hear the murmur of voices now, but was still too far away to make out the words. As she walked, Eva made sure to push her feet right up to the edge of each stair, to stop them from creaking. She crept closer.

About halfway down, the noise from the kitchen became clearer, like a radio dial hitting the right frequency.

'. . . with bad apples in the street, she can't be left alone.' Dad's voice was firm.

Bad apples? Eva wondered what he was talking about. No one had any fruit trees as far as she knew.

'No, I know,' Gran replied. 'But it can't go on like this. Enough is enough.'

'Jaclyn, it isn't your business!' The shout was sudden. It made her jump. The moths in her chest whirled. Were Dad and Gran arguing? They never argued. They were always super-polite to each other all the time.

Gran's answer was quieter. Eva couldn't make it out. She took another careful step. They would both be furious if they knew she was out of bed and listening.

'I think I know what's best for my daughter,' she heard Dad say.

Her. They were talking about her. Eva's mind spun. What had she done? What was the matter? For the last two years she'd been on her best behaviour. They all had, treating each other like delicate china that could crack in an instant. Eva held her breath and finally reached the last step. She sat down on it and leaned in the direction of the open kitchen door.

'She spends her whole time with us. She has no friends her own age. I understand why you worry, but it really isn't healthy.'

'She likes to be with us.' Dad sounded hurt.

'I didn't say she didn't. She's a good girl and I love having her around. You know that. But she needs friends, Martin. People her own age to run around with, getting muddy and bruising her knees and riding bikes.'

'I take her on bike rides. We went last month.'

'I know,' Gran spoke gently. 'You're not listening to me.'

There was a pause. Eva wondered if they had finished talking. She wondered if she should go back upstairs before one of them spotted her.

Then Gran spoke. 'Listen, Martin. I love you both. You know that. I'd do anything for you. But sometimes people don't need to have everything done for them. This would be good for Eva. You have to let her spread her wings a bit. You have to let her take some risks.'

'What, like you did?'

Eva gasped.

Gran must have too, because the next minute Dad was saying sorry, saying he hadn't meant it, that he took it back.

The next time Gran spoke, her voice was thick with tears. 'Just look at it, OK? Think about it. We both want what's best for Eva. And I think this is best.'

Eva wanted to run into the kitchen, to hug Gran and say sorry. She didn't know for what, but she was sorry.

Instead, she stood up and walked gingerly back up to her room.

As she pulled the duvet back over herself, she wondered why they were fighting. And what did it have to do with her?

CHAPTER 4

'I don't see why I can't go to Gran's,' Eva said to Dad.

He pressed his lips together tightly.

'I always go to Gran's,' Eva said.

'I know. But she put her foot down last night. She thinks this is what's best for you.' Dad pushed the leaflet across the kitchen table. 'She wants you to go to this instead.'

The picture of a crooked old house looked scary among the breakfast things: cereal, toast and mortal terror.

Eva glanced at it, but it was always harder to read when she was feeling stressed. And she was feeling super-stressed.

Dad waited for her to try. But she wasn't going to try. She felt her slug-sulk appear. He sighed then picked up the leaflet and began reading.

'*Elizabeth Park Lodge needs you! Every morning over the summer holidays, all local young people are invited to come and help spruce up the former park keeper's lodge. It will become the Elizabeth Park Youth Centre – but only with your help.*' He laid the leaflet down again and stood up. He turned on the radio next to the sink.

'*Burn107FM here to start off your morning with sunshine and music.*'

He turned the radio off again.

'Look, Bug, the thing is, Gran's determined you'll try this. She's said she's only going to look after you in the afternoons from now on. So I need to find somewhere for you to go in the mornings. Starting this morning. It's what's called a *fait accompli*, which is French for dropping me right in it. If you do this today, I can try and find something else for tomorrow. But I can't not go to work. Please, Ladybug. For me?'

He looked tired, Eva thought. What with the McIntyres in one ear and Gran in the other, he probably hadn't had enough sleep.

She would try to be a superhero, she thought, for Dad.

She'd just wear her invisibility shield and everyone would ignore her. It would be OK. She nodded slowly.

Dad breathed a big sigh. 'Thank you,' he said. 'Now,

you're not walking there on your own. Me or Gran will take you and bring you back. And take a cardie. It's warm now, but it might rain later.'

He stepped closer and pulled a hairband from his back pocket. Eva felt him tug her hair into a ponytail. 'This is Gran's idea. But she's not the boss of us. If you hate it, then you don't have to go back. I'll think of something.'

'I don't know anything about building stuff.' Eva winced as he tightened the band.

'I don't think you'll be building. That's all been done. They've just asked for volunteers to help sort out the look of the place – painting and sweeping and stuff like that. They want the people who'll actually use the youth centre to have a say.'

Eva wanted to say she wouldn't be using the centre. The words were dancing on the tip of her tongue. But it wasn't fair on Dad. He was doing his best. He'd always done his best. This was just something she'd have to put up with, one of those things that were meant to be good for her – like muesli and bread with bits in.

She would be brave.

And if she couldn't manage brave then invisible was an excellent Plan B.

Dad led the way to the park. It wasn't far: out of

the cul-de-sac, then left past the tower block that Dad didn't like her walking near on her own, straight along for a bit and through the west gate. The old lodge was near the main gate, so they turned right and walked past the play park.

With each step, Eva felt her heart sink a little lower. She hated strange places and strange people. The sun shone on her face, but didn't reach her insides.

The play park was already a bedlam of toddlers. One bounced back and forth on a sprung chicken. He swayed so wildly that it looked as though the chicken were trying to throw him off. The paths were full of people stomping to work. They had their heads down, earphones in, shoulders bent; grey commas on a green background. They looked like they needed an exclamation mark to pep up their day. She probably looked the same, she realised.

'You don't have to come with me to the lodge. I know the way,' she said to Dad. 'You can carry on to work, if you like.'

Dad held out the crook of his elbow, inviting her to take it. 'I fancy a walk. I spend too much time cooped up indoors. Did you know that human beings do their very best thinking when they're outdoors? True fact, as you might say. It's something to do with not having a ceiling above them smothering their thoughts.'

'Is it?' Eva looked up at the hot-air-balloon sky above them. She knew perfectly well that Dad was trying to distract her. The annoying thing was it worked. Was it really easier to think outdoors than indoors?

'Why are there schools then? Indoors, I mean?'

Dad laughed. 'I'd hate to look after hundreds of children with no walls to keep them in. I'd lose them all in half an hour.'

They were by the main gate now. There were no proper gates any more, though there must have been once. Instead, there was a stumpy pole in the middle of the path to stop cars driving in. The stone gateposts were still there, like two giant thumbs saying 'OK'.

But she wasn't OK.

'You'll be fine,' Dad said.

'If I really hate it, can I stay with Gran tomorrow?' Eva asked. She could hear the panic in her own voice.

Dad didn't answer, but he gave her arm a little squeeze with his own and set off up the lane to the lodge.

Eva kept her eyes down and followed behind him. The tarmac beneath her feet was old and cracked. Tufts of green grass burst from the cracks, like green-haired imps buried feet first. If she dug down just a little bit, she'd see their faces covered in soil.

She reached into her pocket. To most people, her pocket would have seemed empty. But not to Eva. She took out her invisible invisibility shield. She shook out its invisible creases and then swirled it round her shoulders. It landed, lighter than an invisible feather, across her back.

She smiled. That should stop people from bothering her. It was a shield she used a lot at school and people had long ago stopped noticing her. As long as she kept her head down and her voice quiet, then people's eyes just slid right over her as though she really were invisible.

She let her hand drop from Dad's arm.

'Right, Ladybug,' he said. 'Let's get you signed up for a bit of manual labour.'

The old lodge was a big red-brick building. It must have been nice once, but now chipped paint flaked from its windowsills like snowflakes and grass grew in its gutters. There were people outside, a few adults, but mostly groups of children. Eva scanned the faces nervously. She knew one or two from school, but there was no one here from her class. Good. She shrugged her shield higher, to cover her face.

Dad walked towards a young woman who held a

clipboard. She had blonde hair tucked under a pink and purple scarf. She smiled at Dad as he approached. Eva followed reluctantly.

'One more for the cause,' Dad said.

'Great. Will you be staying too?'

Dad shook his head. 'Not today. Work. But maybe another time.'

'OK. I'll just need your daughter to fill out some details. Emergency contact, allergies, that sort of thing.' She held out her clipboard to Eva.

Dad stepped between them. 'Oh, I can take care of that. Why don't you get her working on something? No time like the present.'

Eva flashed a grateful look at Dad while he filled out the form. Her palms had gone sweaty so she wiped them on the back of her jeans.

'Of course,' the young woman said. 'I'm Sally. I'll get you started. Come and meet some of the others.'

'Do you want me to stay a bit?' Dad asked as he scribbled something on the bottom of the form.

Eva shook her head. 'No, it's OK. I'll be OK.'

'Good girl.'

Dad dropped a quick library-stamp kiss on the top of her head, handed the clipboard to Sally and then walked back the way they'd come.

She was on her own. Though she had Sally to follow.

She trotted after her and stopped by her side when they reached the nearest group of children. Sally checked her list.

'Eva, this is, er . . . Shanika, Dilan and Heidi. They're about your age. Maybe you can work with them today?'

Eva nodded a hello. Sally smiled warmly, then moved on to the next group.

The tallest of the children, a girl with long dark hair and a green cotton dress spoke. 'People call me Shan, short for Shanika. My brother gets called Dil. I'm going to ask if our group can do painting. I like painting. Is that OK with you? Heidi doesn't mind – she's already said. It's painting or tidying the garden, and I don't like worms.'

Eva felt a little as though she wanted to run straight after Dad and beg him to let her go to Gran's. But she made herself stand still, because of the *fait accompli*.

'So, we should probably get overalls,' Shan continued, 'or at least aprons, so we don't get paint on our clothes. My mum would go spare if me or Dil came home covered in paint. Though we're wearing work clothes, of course.'

Shan didn't seem to notice that she was the only one talking.

Heidi, who had a round face and huge brown hair,

might have winked at Eva. It was so quick that Eva wasn't sure she'd really seen it. And maybe Heidi had a twitch, maybe it wasn't a wink at all.

'Oh, no,' Shan said, looking over Eva's shoulder. 'Mum would not like this.'

CHAPTER 5

Eva turned to see what Shan was talking about.

It was him. The boy from next door. The McIntyre boy from the shed roof.

'I can't believe he's here,' Shan said. 'Mum says the whole family is bad news. I wonder why he's volunteering?'

The boy wasn't alone. A woman walked beside him, though she didn't look as if she really belonged with him. She wore neatly ironed jeans and a flowery blouse. Rows of purple beads hung round her neck like swags on a Christmas tree. Eva also noticed that her bag looked more like a briefcase than a handbag. They were carrying on a low conversation.

'I'm here, aren't I?' the boy said.

The woman's reply was too quiet to hear.

'I said I would, Mel. Give it a rest.'

A moment later, Sally guided the boy towards Eva's group. She felt her heart speed up a little. Suddenly her shoes were the most interesting thing she'd ever seen.

'I know you,' he said. 'You live next door to me. I've seen you.'

The invisibility shield seemed to crumble and fall away as he looked at her. Eva had to look back. The boy had hazel-brown eyes, flecked with yellow and gold. They were like a cat's eyes, or a tiger's.

'Oh good,' Mel said abruptly. 'A friend. Well, Jamie, I'll be back in two hours. If you need me, I've got my mobile. I just need a quick word with Sally. Try to be good, yeah?'

Eva was sure that her face was fast-car red. *He'd seen her watching*. This had to be the most embarrassing moment ever.

'Jamie,' the boy said. 'I'm Jamie.'

Eva heard a sniff. Shanika.

'I know who you are,' Shanika said. Her voice was as frosty as Eva's face was hot.

Jamie squared his shoulders and lifted his chin higher. 'Yeah? Well, I don't know you. And I don't want to either. I wasn't talking to you.'

'Good.' Shanika grabbed Dilan's shoulder and tugged him towards the lodge. Heidi glanced towards

Shanika, then back to Eva. She gave the smallest of shrugs and then followed Shanika inside.

Eva was left on her own with Jamie. 'I'm Eva,' she said quietly.

He grinned at her. His eyes seemed to sparkle with hidden laughter. 'Eva. Cool. Looks like you're working with me.'

Eva didn't know what to say, so she just nodded.

They stood together for a second, neither speaking. Then Sally was back by their side. Eva let out a small breath that she hadn't even realised she'd been holding.

'Right, Jamie,' Sally said with a wide smile. 'Mel says you're keen to help.'

Jamie gave Eva a quick grin. 'She probably did, yes. She said the same to me.'

'Isn't it true?' Sally asked.

'I'm here. I've got my least-best jeans on and my second-worst pair of trainers. The worst-worst pair got chewed by my dog. So, yes, it looks like I'm all ready for work, doesn't it?'

Sally raised an eyebrow. 'It certainly looks that way. I guess I'll hope for the best then. Shanika's team has taken all the aprons. So you two will be working outside. OK? Grab a bin bag and some gloves and put anything in the bag that you don't think should be out here – rubbish, weeds. If it looks wrong, chuck it.'

Eva took a bag and gloves from Sally's outstretched hands. She wasn't entirely sure that she knew what a weed looked like. Perhaps she'd just stick to old crisp packets and cans. Better to be safe than sorry, as Dad said.

She moved towards the trees. Jamie followed.

As soon as Sally went inside, Jamie dropped the bag and the gloves on the ground. 'Last one to the top is a stink bomb,' he said.

Eva watched as he reached for a low branch and swung himself up. He followed the thick trunk, disappearing into the green canopy above. Lost in an emerald sky.

His voice floated down. 'Sorry to tell you this, Eva, when we've only just met, but it looks like you're the stink bomb.'

'We're supposed to collect rubbish,' Eva said.

'Well, I've found a plastic bag stuck up here. I'll bring it down with me. Come on up – the view's amazing. I can see our street from here.'

Eva glanced back at the lodge. A few children milled around with bin bags, but Sally was nowhere to be seen. She felt the corner of her mouth twitch. She was supposed to be working; she was supposed to be building a youth centre.

She remembered what Gran had said to Dad.

She was supposed to be making friends.

What harm could climbing a tree do?

She folded her bag carefully and put it next to Jamie's with the gloves on top to stop it blowing away. Then she began to climb.

The bark felt coarse and flaky and smelled of earth. Tree skin.

'Hey, what are you waiting for? A written invitation?' Jamie yelled.

'I'm coming!'

She could see him now. He straddled a section where the trunk divided in two. His legs hung down on either side as if he were riding a beach donkey. She stretched up once more, then swung into place beside him. There was just enough room for the two of them to sit in the cleft of the trunk.

'Welcome to the mothership,' Jamie said solemnly.

'The what?'

'This is no ordinary chestnut –'

'I think it might be a sycamore –'

'This is no ordinary tree. This is an organic life form, capable of sustaining living organisms as it travels at the speed of light through galaxies. The oxygen produced by its leaves can sustain us for the years required on our space-exploration mission. The super-jets concealed in its roots will steer us on a safe course through stars as we seek out aliens and make first contact.'

Eva reached her hand towards a knot in the trunk. It was dark and damp with dew. 'I've found the ignition button,' she said, putting her hand over the knot. 'It just needs the fingerprint scans of both pilots.' She smiled. She had played games like this with Mum.

Jamie put his hand beside hers. His fingernails were dark with dirt. Her hands had green smears from something.

'Three, two, one . . . blast off.' Jamie gave a throaty rumble and leaned back, g-forces pushing him against the branch. Eva copied. Sunlight poured through the prisms of green around her, like the comet trails of distant galaxies. Their exploration of the stars had begun.

Jamie dramatically described their route and the aliens they met along the way: green and tall, purple and small, teeth and scales and tails. Each one a new discovery. Eva just had to say 'hello' and come in as Jamie's back-up if the encounters got too dangerous.

She forgot completely about the lodge below.

'Enemy craft moving into range,' Jamie said a while later. He pointed down at the drive.

The enemy craft was the woman he'd arrived with earlier. As she walked, she tapped furiously at the phone she held. Her steps were brisk and purposeful. She wasn't someone who'd climb a tree and save the universe, Eva thought.

'My social worker,' Jamie said. 'Melanie.'

Social worker.

Eva knew a little bit about social workers. One had come to visit her once, two years ago, when they were deciding whether Dad could look after her on his own. She'd been a nice lady, but that hadn't stopped Eva being terrified of her.

'Mel!' Jamie yelled. 'Mel! Up here.'

Melanie stopped at the bottom of the tree. She shielded her eyes as she searched for Jamie. 'Have you actually done any volunteering this morning?' she asked. Her voice was sarcasm central.

'Not exactly,' he said. 'But I made a new friend. Is it time to go?'

'Yes.'

Jamie grinned at Eva. 'See you tomorrow?'

He slithered down the tree like a lizard.

Eva was left to climb down slowly, searching for each branch with the tips of her toes before lowering herself on to it. She'd made a new friend, she thought. It was what Gran wanted.

But Dad would not like it one bit.

CHAPTER 6

Eva rinsed the glasses under the hot tap before balancing them on the draining board. She could see herself reflected in the window behind the sink. There were two of her in the double glazing; overlapping but separate.

She'd felt like two people earlier as well.

Dad had met her at the lodge during his lunch break and walked her round to Gran's.

'Did you make any friends?' he'd asked.

She'd paused. Then she'd said, 'There was a nice girl called Heidi.'

She couldn't tell him about Jamie – he hated the McIntyres. Old Eva would never have kept secrets from Dad. But today it felt like there was a New Eva here too, and that one did.

She reached across the sink and turned the radio on. It made her feel better to have music playing.

Beyond the window, the garden was dusky purple. She could make out shapes that were the humps of bushes and the scaffolding of the swing.

Did something move?

Eva wasn't sure. She leaned up and over the sink. Was there something out there?

She peered into the bruised violet night.

It was probably just a cat.

She breathed out.

Slam!

She leapt back.

A hand was pressed up against the glass. The pads of the fingers were yellow where the pressure pushed the blood away.

Slam!

A second hand joined it. She heard a low moan.

She'd seen a zombie film once, by accident. Dad had turned it off as soon as he'd walked into the room, but not before Eva had heard the moans of the dead. She snatched up one of the empty glasses.

The hands clawed their way up the pane of glass. Then a face appeared below the hands.

Jamie.

Eva let out a shriek of annoyance.

Come out, he signalled.

Eva looked towards the living room. Dad was

watching telly. She heard him laugh at something. She put the glass back. Dashing her hands on her jeans to dry them, she opened the back door.

'What do you think you're doing? You gave me the fright of my life!'

Jamie grinned. 'More interesting than the washing-up though, wasn't it?'

Eva pulled her cardigan round her. Now that the sun had gone down, the summer air was colder. 'You shouldn't do that to people. You'll scare someone to death one day and that will be manslaughter. Or even murder!'

'Don't get upset – it was only a joke.'

'Well, it wasn't funny. What are you doing out here anyway? How did you get into our garden?'

'Easy.' Jamie stepped back from the doorway on to the uneven concrete path. He spun on his heel and pointed to the battered old shed at the bottom. 'Our shed is right next to yours on the other side of the fence. I climbed over.'

Eva stepped out of the kitchen after him. She closed the door behind her. It was best if Dad didn't know Jamie was here. She thought about her double reflection in the window again.

'I noticed it a while ago,' he said quietly. 'I thought it would be easy to get into your garden from ours without going round to the front door. Do you want to see?'

She glanced back at the house. The kitchen was still empty. 'OK, but just for a minute.'

They moved through the twilight. The purple shades were turning navy, and the sky above them was a smear of jam and orange juice.

Jamie moved towards the shed. It had been there for as long as Eva could remember. It had been painted once, but now the paint fell off in big scabs. Dad dragged a lawnmower out a few times a year, but otherwise no one went into it any more.

'I used to play in here, when I was really little,' Eva said softly.

'Yeah?'

'It was a den. Sort of. Mum made cushions and things for me to sit on.'

Jamie stepped up on to a pile of abandoned wood, then pulled himself on to the roof. Eva followed. She'd climbed more in the last two days than she had in all of the last two years put together.

The roof of the shed was rough, like black sandpaper. Tufts of moss grew like continents on a map. Jamie stepped across the narrow gap that separated his shed roof from hers.

'Oh,' she said. 'Weird.' Looking at her house from

this angle, she almost didn't recognise it. Her bedroom window was lit and it cast a soft glow down the back wall, like candlelight. The garden looked like it was hiding secrets – fairies or elves tucked into the rambling leaves of plants. She could almost hear them whispering mysterious spells and incantations. If Jamie turned into a frog right now, she wouldn't have been at all surprised. Well, maybe just a little bit. She felt a shiver of excitement. The gap between the sheds was dark and damp. A really skinny ogre could make a home there. Eva stepped across the space and hoped that no clawed arm shot up and grabbed her ankle.

She arrived on the other side without a monster attached.

'This is your den, isn't it? On the roof? I've seen you lying here,' she said to Jamie.

'I guess. I like it up here. I get some peace.'

'I suppose you need it,' she said cautiously.

'Why? What's that supposed to mean?' Jamie's scowl was easy to see despite the dusk.

'Nothing.' Eva held up her palms. 'I just meant that it does seem a bit . . . loud in your house. You might need to find somewhere quiet sometimes. That's all.'

Jamie's angry expression melted into a grin. 'It does get noisy, doesn't it?'

He sat down on the mossy roof. Eva joined him.

It felt magical. Up above the gardens, hidden away in the fading light. If they stayed really still, they might see the night creatures coming out – the goblins and sprites. Or at least the hedgehogs.

'It's my brothers, mostly,' Jamie said, breaking into her imaginings.

'Your brothers?' Eva wasn't exactly sure which of the many young men she'd seen in next-door's garden were Jamie's brothers.

'Michael and Drew. They're older than me. A lot older. They're grown up, but they still live at home. They like to party, and Mum and Dad don't mind.'

'Do you mind?' Eva asked quietly. She wondered if that was why he always seemed to be hiding, separate from the rest of his family.

Jamie shrugged. 'Your house is different,' he said. 'It's quiet, calm. I think it must be nice, you know, to have your parents there when you come home from school, to have the house tidy and ordered and neat. That's what I imagine, anyway, when I look at your house.'

Eva felt a sudden piercing feeling in her chest. She couldn't answer him.

'Look.' Jamie was pointing up into the sky. 'The first star is out.'

Eva followed his gaze. The red and orange sky had

sunk into inky blue and a bright twinkle of light had appeared.

'Do you know the best thing I ever saw?' Jamie paused to make sure Eva was listening.

Eva found her voice again. 'No, what?'

'Once, where we used to live, there was a power cut. It was night-time and all the lights went out in the houses and the streets. The whole place went as dark as a cave. Mum fished around in the kitchen, looking for candles and banging into things. But I went outside. You could see better in the garden than in the house because of the moon and stars. I climbed a tree. I could see the sky the way it's meant to be. There were so many stars. They were clustered together in a line, like the headlights on a motorway – a go-faster stripe in the sky. That was the Milky Way, I found out later. It was amazing.'

A second star appeared, near to the first.

'And you know the most amazing thing?' Jamie asked.

'No, what?'

'The stars are always there. Even when the lights are on. Even in the daytime. That strip of stars is always there, right above our heads. Millions of them.'

Eva nodded slowly. 'That *is* amazing,' she said.

They watched the sky as another star appeared, then

another, until the pinpricks of light were tossed against the black like glitter on card.

From her own house, Eva heard a shout. 'Eva! Eva!'

She could hear the worry, the panic, in Dad's voice. She had been out too long.

'I have to go.' She kept low over the shed roofs and dropped down into her own garden. She ran into the kitchen and through to the hall.

Dad stood at the bottom of the stairs, his face twisted with anguish.

'Where were you?' he asked. She could see a vein on his neck pulsing hard.

'Just in the garden,' she whispered. 'I'm sorry.'

'I thought . . .' Dad gave a faltering laugh. 'I don't know. I thought you'd been stolen away. That the elves had taken you. I'm sorry. I shouldn't have panicked.' He gave her a hug, pulling her into him with strong arms. 'I couldn't bear it if something happened to you,' he said. 'We're all we've got now. You know that, don't you? It's me and you.'

Eva knew that.

But there was a part of her that wished she'd been able to stay to watch all the stars come out.

CHAPTER 7

Eva and Jamie weren't on litter duty the next morning. Instead, they had got their hands on some paintbrushes and were part of Shanika's team. Jamie muttered that Shanika should be collecting litter, seeing as they'd done it yesterday. It was only fair to swap. Eva blushed – they hadn't actually picked up any litter.

'Here's an apron,' Shanika said.

'Thanks.' It was firework-splattered with paint. Eva slipped it over her head.

'What about me?' Jamie asked.

'That was the last one,' Shanika said, though she didn't seem at all sad about it. 'Maybe you'd better help outside, after all.'

'No, it's fine. I'm wearing old clothes.'

Shanika glanced up and down. 'Evidently.'

Eva wasn't sure if Jamie was being insulted or not,

but, by the way he squared his shoulders, he obviously thought he was. Shanika walked away, following Sally.

They would be painting the main room of the lodge. It was going to be the heart of the club, with squidgy sofas, a pool table and computers. Right now it looked more like a building site. Well, a building site and furniture shop. Actually, a building site, furniture shop and sports centre, all chucked in a big blender and whizzed around. There were piles of wood, bags of plaster and towers of bricks. Desks balanced on top of each other, and stacks of chairs wobbled worryingly. Two five-a-side goals and some hockey sticks jostled for space.

'A work in progress then?' Jamie said, looking at the mess.

There was one long, blank wall that was the perfect canvas for a mural.

Yesterday's crew had made a good start. The mural was the outside come inside. There was the lodge and the park around it, a baby-blue sky above with sheep-ish clouds, the hill in the middle of the park with its lumpy slopes and the whole town in miniature beyond with its rows and rows of houses and shops and offices.

Most of the park had been painted, but the town was still just a pencil sketch waiting for the colours to bring it to life.

Eva couldn't help smiling. It was going to be great. A proper work of art, something you could look at again and again. She hoped she could put her and Dad on their street. Playing a game, maybe, the way they used to.

'The paint is all ready,' Sally said. 'Shan came in early to mix it – thank you, Shan. Just try to stay inside the lines. Best you can, anyway. I'll be in the office, if you need me, trying to get donors to give us more equipment.'

Jamie scowled at Shanika who was busy handing out pots of colour. Eva hoped she'd get to do their street. Or maybe the hill with all the dogs on, or a bit of sky with kites sailing through.

'You two,' Shan said, 'here's some white and black. You can do the roads. And the pavements and the zebra crossings.'

Jamie didn't take the pots that Shanika held out to him.

Shanika sighed, then swivelled slightly and offered the pots to Eva.

Eva found she was holding them, though she wasn't sure that she had taken them.

'Roads are the most boring bits,' Jamie said.

'Well, someone has to do them. Or do you think your contribution yesterday was enough?'

Eva nipped her bottom lip. Shanika had a point.

They hadn't done any work at all yesterday. They should make up for it today. 'It's all right,' she said, 'I don't mind.'

She took a brush from the pile on the floor and began painting.

She could feel Jamie's sulk. He was as miserable as cold rice pudding three days old. He didn't pick up a paintbrush.

'If Shanika thinks I'm painting any stupid roads with stupid paint, then she has another stupid think coming. I won't do it, especially not without an apron. I want an apron.'

Eva felt the corner of her mouth twitch. Jamie sounded like a toddler.

'Don't laugh,' he snapped. 'There's nothing wrong with wanting an apron.'

'Sorry, you just sound funny.'

'You didn't think I sounded funny last night, when I told you about the stars. You listened to me then.'

'I know. It was interesting.'

'More than this stupid mural is. Hey, I've got an idea. Give me the white.'

Eva handed over the paint.

Jamie picked up a long, tapering paintbrush from the pile and began to stir the paint as if it were tea.

'We're made from stars. Did you know that?' he

said. 'The Big Bang sent out millions and billions of atoms that got sucked up together to make millions of suns. And all the atoms in the whole universe were once part of a star like our sun. There are bits of stars everywhere. I'm looking at one right now.'

He was looking right at her with a lopsided grin.

'I'm not a star,' Eva whispered.

'You are, we all are. We can't help it. There are stars everywhere!' he said. 'Here!' He moved the paintbrush over the mural. 'And here! And here!' With every word, he painted a rough star shape on the wall. Five quick strokes that glooped and dribbled over the sky and hill and park. 'Here! Here! Here!' The streets and shops and roads were all daubed. 'Here,' Jamie said, and painted a white star on the lodge.

When he'd finished, he was panting.

Everyone looked at him, stunned.

'What have you done?' Shanika asked. 'You've ruined it. I'm telling!'

Shanika flounced out of the room, obviously on her way to tell Sally.

'I'd better get out of here,' Jamie said.

'No. Stay. Explain. They won't mind.'

He raised an eyebrow at her. 'Of course they will. They always mind when you don't do as they tell you. Don't you know that?'

He put the pot of paint down and handed her his paintbrush. 'Just say you didn't notice what I was doing. You won't get into trouble then.'

Before Eva could answer, Jamie had pulled his hood up over his head and banged open the emergency exit. He turned left into the park, then he was gone.

Eva gripped the paintbrush. There was a row coming – she knew it; it was like the metal taste of the sky when a storm was on the way. She wished she could wave the brush, like a wand, and whip the stars away. The white points were dripping down now, small streams of paint ruining the rest of the design.

Why had he done it?

Why?

Shanika's voice came from the corridor, shouting for Sally.

The storm was nearly here.

Eva dropped the paintbrush on a sheet of newspaper and followed Jamie though the exit.

Outside, the sun felt warm on her skin and the sound of shouting was replaced by birdsong and the yells of a game of frisbee.

Jamie was nearly out of sight, right at the end of the drive. Was he going home?

'Jamie!' she yelled. 'Wait!'

He paused, looked back, then waved to her quickly
– *Run!*

She ran until she caught up with him. 'Where are you going?' she asked.

He grinned. 'Just making myself scarce. Are they looking for me yet?'

She nodded.

'So, looks like my painting and decorating days are over. It's all right – I didn't like it anyway. It's time for Plan B. This way!' Jamie set off at a sprint.

'What's Plan B?' Eva yelled, chasing after him. But he just laughed. It was a sound without walls. A sound as free as the birdsong. Eva paused, just for a moment. Dad would hate this. She knew he would. *I won't leave the park*, she promised Dad silently, then she ran after Jamie.

He turned left at the drive, heading away from the main gate. She followed. The hill rose up in front of them, but Jamie turned left again, avoiding the rise. Instead he ran past the pinging basketball courts, past a ragged football match and on towards the play park. Eva was out of breath when she caught up with him at the swings. In seconds, he'd grabbed the chains of one and launched himself into the sky. She took the swing next to him and stretched her feet higher and higher. Her hair trailed out behind her like a comet's tail.

'To infinity and beyond!' Jamie yelled, and leapt from the swing just as it reached the top of its flight. He was all arms and legs, flailing like a thrown spider. Then he landed on the squishy surface in a roll and a crash.

Eva dragged the soles of her feet against the ground, slowing herself with a jolt. 'Are you OK?'

Jamie sat up and rubbed his elbow. 'Yeah, of course I'm OK. I've got rubber knees and elastic elbows, my mum says. Do you want an ice cream?'

The van was parked at the edge of the playground. It was square and boxy with a window set in the side. The fading stickers surrounding the window showed ice lollies and cones with prices written on in marker pen.

'You want to buy an ice cream?' she asked. She didn't have any money. Dad was going to meet her to walk her home at lunchtime.

'Not buy it, no.'

Eva gripped the chains of the swing. 'You don't want to steal it, do you?'

Jamie flashed her an angry look. 'No. Of course not.' Then he grinned. 'Probably not.'

Eva followed as he stepped up to the van. The man behind the counter wore what had once been a white coat, but it had long given up the fight against strawberry sauce and chocolate ripple and was now covered in stains. The man, and his coat, both looked a bit fed up. As Jamie approached, he didn't smile.

'What can I get you, son?' he asked.

Jamie put his hands on his hips like a cowboy.

'The chance to fulfil a lifelong dream,' Jamie said.

'Well, I've never heard a ninety-nine described quite so enthusiastically,' the man said.

'Ninety-nines, wafer cones, spirals, screwballs with a bubble-gum at the bottom, orange lollies, choc ices and fizzy pop.'

'Is that your order?' The man grinned.

'No. That is a list of the awe and wonder you have at your fingertips because of this magical van. And that machine.' Jamie pointed to the ice-cream maker that was fixed to the left of the man. It was square, silver and had a nozzle dripping vanilla ice cream into a tray beneath.

'Oh,' the man said, looking a bit baffled.

'Today is my birthday,' Jamie said. 'I won't lie to you, I've had some great presents already. I'm lucky. I know that. I had a twelve-speed bike and a new game for my PS3. But what I didn't get was a go on the most beautiful invention known to man. That machine.'

Jamie paused. The man was smiling now. 'It's your birthday, is it, son?'

'Yeah.'

'What star sign are you?'

'Star sign?'

'Yes, you know, Gemini, Leo, Taurus. If it's your birthday today, which one are you?'

'What's the lucky one, where people give you what you want when you ask nicely? I'm that one.'

The man laughed. 'OK. You're on. Who am I to ruin your birthday? Come round to the door.'

Jamie grabbed Eva's arm and rushed her towards the side. It was already open to get a breeze going through on this hot morning. The man stood in the doorway.

'I'm Brian,' he said. 'Don't tell anyone I let you do this. I'd lose my job.'

'Brian,' Jamie said solemnly, 'I'm Jamie and that's Eva and we will take this to our graves. Won't we, Eva?'

Eva nodded.

Brian stood aside to let them get in. The inside of the van smelled like sugar and milk, with a hint of engine oil. Eva felt herself shiver, though she wasn't sure if that was from excitement or from the freezer she was resting against.

'What do I do?' Jamie asked.

'Well, it's very technical,' Brian said. 'It takes years as an apprentice and lots of training and practice. See that handle?' He pointed to the ice-cream machine.

'Pull it down. Put something underneath to catch the ice cream.'

Jamie grabbed the cone that Brian held out. He put it under the nozzle then pulled down. Ice cream shot out in whirls of creamy gloop. The cone filled up, and up, until it spilled over the sides and on to Jamie's fingers. The stream kept on coming. Jamie tried to catch it with his arm, but it glooped everywhere.

'I told you it was an art form,' Brian said. He leaned over and flipped up the handle. He turned to Eva. 'Think you can do a better job?'

She nodded.

She was much more gentle. She eased the handle down and let the stream fall smoothly into the cone. When it was full, she flipped up the handle and her cone finished in a stiff point.

'Beautiful,' Brian said. 'Flake?'

She nodded and he popped a flake into the top.

Jamie sucked the ice cream off his arm and stuffed the cone into his mouth. Eva took a few licks of hers. It was cool and delicious and tasted like summer. Jamie's was gone in a few mouthfuls. He tipped up the wafer point to get the last of it to run down his throat.

'One more go?' he asked hopefully.

Brian shrugged. 'As it's your birthday. And you could do with the practice.'

Jamie didn't take a cone this time. Instead he moved quickly. He dipped his head and twisted his neck so that his mouth was under the nozzle.

'Oi!' Brian said, and reached out quickly.

Not quick enough.

Jamie pulled the nozzle down as far as it would go. His face seemed to explode in a burst of cream. It overran his mouth, slid on to his chin and cheeks and puddled in his dimples.

Brian grabbed him by the shoulder and hoisted him away. Ice cream poured on to the floor. Eva pushed the handle up and scurried after Brian, who held Jamie aloft like a stray cat. 'Out!' he yelled.

He dropped Jamie on the floor outside the van. He sprawled on the grass. Eva followed more gingerly.

'Sorry,' she said to Brian. 'Thanks for letting us have a go.'

'*You* can come back,' he said. 'But that one is barred. Give some people an inch and they'll take a mile, do you know that?'

Jamie leaned against Eva, wiping ice cream from his eyes and nose. His mouth was clamped closed and his cheeks were puffed out with all the frozen cream he could keep in there. He was trying not to laugh.

Finally he swallowed it all down. 'Ow!' He clutched

the side of his head. 'Ice-cream headache. Still, that was worth it, wasn't it? That was fun!'

It had been fun.

But she had been away from the lodge for too long. The sun was high in the sky now, and people were sitting on the grass, eating their packed lunches.

Dad would be on his way to the lodge to collect her and she was here with Jamie instead.

Dad wouldn't care that she'd been having fun.

He wouldn't be happy at all.

CHAPTER 8

'I should go back,' Eva said urgently. If she rushed, maybe Dad wouldn't find out that she'd left the lodge.

Jamie shrugged. He sauntered back towards the swings.

'You should come with me,' Eva continued. 'I have to go right now. Will you come with me?'

'No. Maybe tomorrow, if I feel like it. But if I go back now, I'll just get a row. It's the holidays. They should give me a break.'

'But I have to go back,' Eva said. 'My dad will be worried.'

'Will he? Why?'

'He just will.'

'OK, but I want one more go on the swings. I'll see you tomorrow.' He grinned at her. His eyes were a mix of browns and yellows, like a cat in sunshine.

She had no choice. She had to go back by herself.

The sun was right above her, shortening all the shadows. Her own shadow was right beneath her, a dark body walking upside down – touching hers on the soles of her feet. A second Eva. It made her feel uncomfortable.

She turned up the drive towards the lodge.

Oh.

Dad was there already.

She was too late.

He sat on the steps outside the lodge. He held his head in his hands. Sally stood by him. As Sally reached out to touch his shoulder, he pulled away violently.

This looked bad.

'Dad!' Eva called.

His head lifted. His face looked pale and drawn, even at this distance.

Eva broke into a trot. 'Dad!'

Dad got to his feet slowly, as though he was ten years older than he'd been that morning.

He walked towards her. Sally hovered at his side, ready to hold him if he needed it.

'Eva.' He swayed slightly, but kept moving. 'Eva!'

When she got close, it was easy to see how frightened he was. His skin was clammy, despite the warm breeze. His hands were shaking as they reached for her.

Eva held him tight. Willing him to be OK.

He stepped back, out of her arms. 'You left. People saw you leave after that boy. That McIntyre boy.'

Eva felt herself redden. 'Yes. He was upset. I had to –'

'You *had* to stay here. I told you. I made it clear, didn't I? You weren't to leave until me or your gran came to collect you.'

'I'm sorry, I wasn't –'

'You weren't what? You weren't listening? You weren't interested?' His voice got louder with every word.

Sally stepped closer. She was frowning, looking from Eva to Dad, then back again. 'Martin,' she said, laying her hand on Dad's arm. 'Martin, are you OK? Do you need a minute?'

He shrugged her off. He looked as though he were going to say something, but instead he drew a clipped breath and held up his hands.

'OK,' Sally said slowly. 'OK. She's back safe and sound. That's the main thing.' Sally turned to look directly at Eva. 'Your dad's right. You shouldn't leave here while you're in our care. Do you understand that?'

Eva nodded. She felt her cheeks flare. Of course she knew – she just hadn't been thinking when she did it.

'Eva . . .' Sally paused and glanced at Dad again.

'How much do you know about Jamie?'

'Not much,' she answered.

'His life's a bit tricky. Melanie told me a few things. I won't go into it. You seem to be a very sensible girl. But, the thing is, it would be better if you rubbed off on Jamie, not the other way round.'

'What do you mean?'

Dad stepped between Sally and Eva. He put his hand heavily on Eva's shoulder and held her tight. 'That's enough,' he said to Sally. 'Stop it. My daughter is not some pawn for your social worker, or a babysitter for that boy. She's been through enough. What she needs is security. Her family. Me. She won't be having anything more to do with him. Not here, not at home, nowhere.'

He turned his back on Sally. 'We're going home,' he said to Eva. 'And you'll not be seeing that boy again. Is that understood?' He strode down the drive. The shaking had left his hands. They were pulled into tight fists.

'Jamie wouldn't hurt me,' Eva said, trying her best to keep up with Dad's long strides.

'He has already. He made you leave, didn't he? You'd have done as I said if he hadn't interfered. You'd have been safe.'

I was safe, Eva wished she could say. *I was having fun.* Brian and the ice cream seemed like it had happened to someone else. The shadow girl.

53

'I don't want you to see him again. Am I making myself clear?'

He was.

Eva didn't know what to say to make him change his mind. She nodded carefully, answering the last question only.

CHAPTER 9

That night, Eva dreamed of a snowy silence and Dad walking across ice. She tried to struggle awake more than once, but the dream kept sucking her back. It was harsh and cold. Finally she forced her eyes open and lay in the darkness, tangled in her sheets.

In her dream, Dad had been walking away from her.

And that's how it felt in real life too.

Eva kicked off her covers.

It wasn't fair, Eva thought. Dad didn't know Jamie. He had never even spoken to him.

It wasn't fair.

The thought twirled and swirled in Eva's mind like a snowstorm. *Dad wasn't fair.*

She must have gone back to sleep, because the next thing she knew she was woken by a sound that she couldn't place. The light in her room was milky, the colours all different shades of grey. It was still early, really early in the morning.

The sound came again. It was a muffled thud and it came from outside. Eva pushed herself out of bed and peeked through the curtains.

She swallowed a squeal.

A trainer hovered just outside the window pane. It was attached to a long pole, she realised. The pole swung and the trainer bashed against the glass again. She scrabbled with the window catch and pushed it open.

'Morning!' Jamie said. He was hanging out of his own bedroom window, the pole and the trainer gripped tightly in his hands.

Eva rubbed her eyes.

'I thought you might be awake. I had a feeling.'

'Of course I'm awake,' Eva snapped. 'That's what happens when people throw shoes at your window.'

Jamie laughed. 'What are you doing?'

'Nothing. Sleeping.'

'Do you want to see something funny?'

'Now?'

'Yes, now. Can you come out?'

Eva yawned and stretched. The pale morning sun was warm on her skin.

'I can't,' she said. She wasn't even supposed to be talking to Jamie. 'Dad said . . .' She paused. He was smiling so warmly that she couldn't tell him what Dad had said – that they were banned from being friends. She was never, never, to spend time with him. Jamie was a bad influence. A bad apple. A bad boy.

He waved the trainer at her again. His gold-brown eyes looked eager.

'Dad said . . .' she tried again.

'Is your dad awake?' Jamie interrupted.

'No. What time is it?'

'Six thirty. In the morning,' Jamie added helpfully.

Dad wouldn't be awake for half an hour. Eva thought about her dream. *It wasn't fair.*

'Will we be long?' Eva asked.

'Ten minutes. Tops. Promise.'

'Are you sure?'

'Meet me out front.'

The trainer was reeled in, and Jamie's head disappeared.

Eva pulled on a pair of jeans and threw a cardie over her nightie. Her sandals were waiting neatly beside her chair.

On the landing, she paused. She shouldn't go out. Not without telling Dad.

Eva held the banister, not sure which way she should go.

There was no chance that Dad would let her go out. He would send her back to her room and lock the door and the windows. He would stop her going to the lodge. He'd stop her going anywhere ever again.

That seemed to decide it for her legs. They took her down to the front door. She pulled off the chain, turned the key, drew the bolt and stepped outside.

Jamie was already waiting by the front gate.

She pulled the door closed behind her as gently as she could so as not to wake Dad.

Outside felt delicious. The air was cool, but with the smell of sunshine that meant they would be in for a scorching day. She did up the buttons of her cardie and stepped into the low rays of light.

'What did you want to show me?' she asked Jamie.

He grinned. 'I'm glad you came out.'

Eva started to get impatient. 'Why exactly am I here and not still fast asleep?'

'Come with me.' Jamie stepped on to the pavement and began walking away from the house.

'What? Wait! Where are you going?'

'Come on, I'll show you. It's the funniest thing ever.' He took hold of her wrist and pulled gently.

Eva glanced back at her house. It was still, the curtains drawn like closed eyes. Dawn warmed the bricks and made the glass golden. She had a little while before Dad woke up.

'OK, but I can't be long. Dad will worry.'

'We won't be. I promise.'

The streets were deserted. The tweets and chirrups of small birds cheerleading the dawn were the only sounds. It was as if she and Jamie were the only people left in the whole world. For a giddy moment, Eva imagined wandering the sweet aisles of abandoned shops, driving red sports cars through empty streets, doing anything and everything she wanted without any grown-ups to say no. Then she heard the clink and trundle of a milk float and the world came back with a thump – ah well, it was a nice daydream while it lasted.

Jamie was heading towards the park. At the west gate, he turned right.

'Are we going to the lodge? Why?' Eva asked.

'Shh. No. Not the lodge. This way.' Jamie crouched down low, as if he didn't want to be spotted. Eva copied, though she had no idea who they were hiding from. The park had to be deserted at this time of day.

But it wasn't.

There was a group of people on the playing field, loads of them, in tracksuits and trainers and sweat bands. A whole gang of sweaty, puffing, groaning grown-ups.

'What are they doing?' Eva whispered.

Some of the group ran up and down, lifting their

knees as if they were crossing hot coals barefoot. Others rolled on the grass, crunching their stomach muscles and huffing with the dust and the effort. Another group held huge Thor Hammers and were laying into some innocent car tyres with them. The car tyres just took it patiently.

Beside her, Jamie started to giggle.

Eva felt herself smiling too. Grown-ups could be very strange sometimes.

Jamie ducked down behind a bush. His face and hands were dappled with leaf shadow, making him seem camouflaged.

'It's a boot camp,' Jamie explained. 'They do it every morning.' He pulled aside a branch so that they could get a better view. 'You know the best bit?'

'No, what?'

'Look at that one there. The one in the pink tracksuit.'

Eva peered out. Then laughed. She slapped her hand over her mouth so that the adults wouldn't hear her.

Melanie. The woman in the pink tracksuit slamming hammers into tyres at the crack of dawn was Melanie, Jamie's social worker.

A dog leapt around her feet, trying, it seemed, to get right in the way of the hammer. Melanie was trying just as hard to make sure he didn't. They were both getting a good workout.

'That's her dog. Bandit,' Jamie said. 'She drives up here every other morning and tries not to hit Bandit with a hammer. And she thinks I've got problems.'

A tall man wearing army clothes walked from one group to another. He spoke in a clipped, strong voice, but they were too far away to make out the words.

'That's Gary,' Jamie said. 'He's in charge. He used to be a soldier, but now he shouts at civilians for money.' Jamie sounded impressed, though Eva wasn't sure whether it was Gary being a soldier, or Gary making money from shouting at people that impressed him. Maybe both.

Eva settled back on her heels. The sun was a little higher now and the bush they were in cast a long shadow on the grass, like an ogre leaning forward.

'Jamie,' she said, 'why does Melanie look after you?'

'She doesn't look after me, no matter what she thinks. I take care of myself.'

'Yes, but why is she there at all? You've got a family. Loads of them. Why have you got a social worker too?'

Jamie frowned and tugged a leaf off the bush. He started tearing it into strips. 'Mostly *because* of my family, I suppose. Michael and Drew went into care, ages ago, but it means Mel has to keep an eye on me. She's looking for any reason to take me away from Mum and Dad. I know she is. But it's not going to happen. I'll never let it happen. She can't take me away.'

'Why were they in care and not you?'

Jamie let the leaf fall like rain. 'I wasn't born yet. Mum and Dad . . . they had problems . . . I don't know what really, they don't talk about it much. Dad went away, I know that. So Michael and Drew went too. Mum couldn't manage on her own.'

Why would parents go away? There was only one reason that Eva knew, but it couldn't be that.

She must have looked confused, because Jamie said, 'I mean he was in prison.'

Eva felt her face flush. Oh. Her eyes darted to the ground. All she could see were the torn bits of leaf.

'Are you shocked?' There was scorn in Jamie's voice. 'Just because your life is perfect, doesn't mean everyone else's is.'

'My life's not perfect!' Eva said hotly. 'You don't know the first thing about my life.'

'It looks fine from where I'm standing.'

Could she say? Could she do it? Eva held the words in her mouth like a bad taste. She hadn't said them for a long time. She hadn't needed to; she hadn't met anyone new since it had happened.

'My mum died,' she said quietly.

Now it was Jamie's turn to look shocked. 'Really?' he said, in the end.

'Really.'

'How? When?' He looked interested. He leaned towards her so that she could see the yellow and gold in his eyes.

'An accident. Two years ago. A skiing accident.'

'Skiing?' Jamie said it as if it were an idea he couldn't fit anywhere in his head.

Eva took a deep breath. The air tasted of grass clippings and earth and warmth. It tasted of life here and now, not that time two years ago when the world had splintered and broken. 'They went on holiday, Mum and Dad, for their ten-year anniversary. I stayed with Gran, so it would be just them. I remember crying when they drove away. I waved from the doorstep for ages, until Gran made me go inside.'

Jamie's eyes were wide as chocolate coins. 'What happened?'

'Gran told me what happened. Dad wouldn't ever really talk about it. Gran told me that Mum loved to ski. She was always good at things like that. Brave. Anyway, they'd been told that one of the slopes was closed. It was too dangerous, the snow was too thick. But Mum laughed and said it was the best run and they should do it anyway. Dad said no, but she teased him. She went on her own in the end. Dad was right though – she shouldn't have done it.'

Eva paused. She didn't know if she should say the last thing. The thing that Gran hadn't said, but that Eva had realised. The thing that was a dark, dirty thought inside her and Dad both.

Jamie reached out and laid his hand on top of hers. His nails were black with soil, but his palm was warm.

'The worst thing,' Eva whispered, 'the worst is that it wasn't an accident, really. If she'd listened, she wouldn't have died.'

'You think it was her own fault?'

Eva felt the dark twisty idea, like a worm in her skull. It made her want to scrub her insides clean. 'If she'd listened to Dad, it would have been different,' she said softly.

Jamie moved his hand away and reached for another leaf to tear. 'Is that why your dad's so . . . I don't know . . . so odd?'

Eva frowned. 'He's not odd.'

'He is a bit,' Jamie said. 'Complaining about my family all the time. Not letting you go out, wondering where you are every minute of –'

'He just wants to keep me safe,' Eva interrupted.

'He just wants to keep you a prisoner, more like.'

'That's not true!' Eva stood up. 'It isn't! You don't know anything about him. He's kind and funny and he looks after me.'

'Don't shout at me,' Jamie said.

'I can if I want!' Eva shouted.

'No, I mean it. Mel will hear.'

Eva glanced across at the boot camp. No one was looking their way. 'You don't care about me or my dad. All you care about is not getting caught. My dad was right about you,' Eva said. 'Stay away from me, Jamie. Just leave me alone.'

CHAPTER 10

Dad was still asleep when Eva slipped back into the house. She closed the front door behind her and leaned against the wood. It felt strong and solid; she let her shoulder blades press back on it. She could feel tears burning her eyes. How could Jamie say those things about Dad? Jamie knew nothing. She had the best dad in the world. He'd do anything for her. He might fuss a tiny bit, but it was only because he wanted what was best for her.

And she had gone out without telling him with the one person she'd been forbidden from seeing.

Eva's face burned with shame.

She'd let Dad down, and for what? For a stupid boy who didn't care about her.

She dashed the back of her hand against her face. She wouldn't cry, she wouldn't.

Eva went into the kitchen and filled a glass with water. It was icy cold and as she sipped it she felt the cold spread down her chest and into her stomach. Her breathing settled into a calmer rhythm.

When the glass was empty, she rinsed it and put it on the draining board. Then she flipped the switch on the kettle.

She'd make a cup of tea and take it up to Dad. She hadn't done that for ages. Not since school had broken up. Cup, tea bag, water, milk. Then the careful walk upstairs, holding the mug steady with only a few tiny spills that no one would notice.

Eva stopped outside his room. 'Dad?' she whispered. She leaned on the door handle with her elbow. 'Dad?'

Inside, Dad was a hillock of duvet. He groaned and rolled over. His hair was sticking up in a hedgehog head. She put the mug down gently on the bedside table.

'I've brought you tea.'

'Morning, Ladybug.' His voice sounded croaky, full of sleep. 'Is it time to get up? Feels early.'

'It is early, but I was awake.'

Dad eased himself up on his elbows and dragged a palm across his face like a wet flannel. He had a rash of stubble on his chin that rasped against his hand. 'You OK, Bug? You sound funny.'

Eva felt a lump rise in her throat. She swallowed to get rid of it. It didn't work.

'Come and sit down while I drink my tea.'

She perched on the side of his bed, then kicked off her sandals and swung her feet on to the duvet. She folded her legs up so her chin rested on her knees.

'What's up, Bug?'

There was a long pause. Dad took a sip from his cup.

'I was just thinking . . . about Mum,' Eva said.

'Oh.' Dad looked properly awake now. His frowning eyebrows pulled his whole face downwards. 'I see,' he said. He took another careful sip.

Eva pulled her knees tighter. She wasn't sure how to say what she was feeling. Not without mentioning Jamie, anyway. And she definitely didn't want to mention Jamie.

'I wondered . . . I wondered, do you still miss her?'

Dad put the cup down on his bedside table. He slept in the middle of his double bed, so he had to turn away from her to reach it. He took a moment to turn back.

'Where has this come from?' he said finally.

'I was just thinking about her this morning. I got . . . I got cross.'

'With her?' Dad looked concerned.

'No. At least, I don't think so.' She'd been cross

with Jamie, hadn't she? It was him saying that Dad was weird that had made her lose her temper. And yet there was a part of her that was angry with Mum. The dark idea worming inside her.

'Your gran says that anger is part of grieving,' Dad said.

'Is it?'

'I don't know. They say so. Counsellors and people like that.'

'Are you angry?' Eva whispered.

'I haven't got time to be angry. I've got you to worry about. Jaclyn thinks we should all give in to our emotions and let it all hang out. But she always was a free spirit and that just leads to trouble in the end.'

'Gran?' Eva was confused. Was Gran a free spirit? Maybe that's why she wore so much purple.

Dad looked suddenly ashamed. 'I didn't mean anything by that. Your gran has helped me out a lot – I know that. We just disagree sometimes, that's all.'

Eva wished she'd never said anything. Dad looked so worn and tired. She'd wanted to bring him tea. She should have left it at that. Her eyes felt hot again.

'Oh, Bug. Look at you.' Dad smiled a sad smile. 'You're a wet weekend. Come here.' He reached out and pulled her into a hug. She smelled his warm, sleepy skin and fought against her tears.

'I didn't mean to make you cry,' he said. 'I'm a fool. But I'm your fool. You've got me. You know that, don't you?'

Eva nodded. She had Dad and she didn't care what Jamie thought. She didn't care at all.

CHAPTER 11

Dad wasn't sure that Eva should go to the lodge that morning; he was worried that she was too upset. He said he'd call Gran and ask her to have her instead. But Eva said no. Gran wouldn't like it. Gran wanted her to spread her wings. Eva had insisted on going.

But just because she was at the lodge didn't mean she was going to speak to Jamie. It was easy to avoid him, because he was working under supervision. Melanie sat in the main hall. Her briefcase rested on a pile of bricks and she scribbled notes across pages. She had one eye on Jamie though. He was fixing the mural he'd ruined the day before.

Eva took one look and asked Sally if she could work outside again.

'Yes, of course. Heidi and Dilan are in the outdoor gang today. You can work with them,' Sally said.

She moved along the corridor, which was dark and clammy like a cave, and stepped out into bright sunshine. Heidi squealed a little when she noticed Eva.

'I'm glad we got someone else,' Heidi said. 'We're clearing the path today, so we don't have to walk in the road and more hands make light work, my mum always says. And the path needs a ton of work.'

She waved her hand towards the trees. Eva couldn't see a path.

Heidi grinned. 'It's overgrown. But we've got some of those cutty things, seca-wotsits.'

'Hedge scissors?' Eva suggested.

'Hedge scissors! You're funny.' Heidi slipped her arm through Eva's and led her to the pile of tools. There was something about Heidi that reminded Eva of a china doll. She looked as if her eyes would click shut if you tipped her flat.

Dilan was there already, handing out sacks and bright yellow jackets and rakes and anything else he could find to the group that had gathered. There were six volunteers altogether. Eva smiled shyly at the three she didn't know. A couple said hello.

'Right,' Dilan said with purpose. 'You see that path?'

He pointed at a hedge.

'No,' Heidi said.

'Well, by lunchtime, you will,' Dilan said.

Eva could just about make out where the path used to be – the leaves were thinner and light filtered through in whorls, like a giant's fat thumbprint on the hedge-line. Once upon a time it had been an arch through the hedge, a shortcut to the rest of the park.

She picked up a pair of seca-wotsits and started cutting.

The hedge was a hundred-year-old bramble, thick as a dragon's leg, wound round the palace of a sleeping princess.

Eva was a prince, cutting the brambles back, forcing a way through. *Here I come, my lady,* Eva thought as another slice of privet hit the ground. *I'll rescue you.* The heat on her skin was the breath of the sleeping dragon. The dust and dirt and old spiders' webs was the build-up of a hundred years of dreaming.

Eva raised her sword and hacked some more. The princess would soon be free, she thought with a smile.

'Eva,' a voice called, cutting through her daydream.

Shanika.

What did she want?

Eva wiped her face with the back of her sleeve. She felt hot and sweaty, but at least she hadn't woken any sleeping dragons.

'Eva!'

'I'm here.'

Shanika was holding a clipboard and pen. 'I'm going to do some publicity,' she said. 'I can't believe no one has done it before. Local press, that kind of thing. Anyway, I need everyone to write a few words about why they're here.'

'No,' Eva said, shaking her head. 'I don't want to be in the paper.'

'It will just take you a few minutes. It doesn't have to be a novel. Just a few sentences.'

'I said no,' Eva said, a bit more forcefully than she meant to. 'I don't want to. I hate all that stuff.'

Shanika frowned. 'All what stuff?'

Words, Eva thought, words and letters and the maze they made on a page, the way that they slipped out of focus the longer you looked at them, like a photo taken too quickly. The way they slipped out of her mind like wet fish sliding off a plate. The whole stupid soup of words.

'You know,' Shanika said, 'you can be a bit weird sometimes. I think you've been hanging out with that McIntyre boy too much. It's rubbing off on you. Don't worry about your story. I can get plenty of other people to do it. People who want to help. It doesn't bother me.' She turned on her heel and stalked back towards the lodge. Her ponytail whipped back and forth like the tail of an angry cat. Eva could nearly hear her hiss.

She suddenly felt tired. Tired of painting and cutting and moving stuff. Her arms were heavy and her eyes felt full of dust and grit. But she felt tired inside too. First Jamie had nagged her about Dad and now Shanika was having a go at her. Eva had had enough.

She put her secateurs back on the pile of tools and went to wait for Gran.

CHAPTER 12

Everyone was streaming out of the lodge by the time Gran arrived to walk Eva home. Eva was wearing her invisibility shield again. She kept her head down and the collar up and everyone just walked straight past her. She didn't see Jamie leave, though he must have because Sally closed the door of the lodge behind the last volunteer.

As soon as Eva saw Gran walking up the drive with her bag-for-life swinging at her side, she ran towards her and wrapped her in a hug.

'Whoa. What's up, duck?' Gran asked.

'Nothing,' Eva mumbled into her sweatshirt.

'Well, it's the most something-looking nothing that I've ever seen. Did you row with someone?'

Had she?

Not a row, exactly. It was just Shanika who had

made her feel stupid and small. And Jamie who had made her cry that morning, though he hadn't meant to. And Dad. Eva was surprised to find that she was cross at Dad too, though she wasn't sure why.

She didn't answer Gran; she just buried herself deeper in the scent of Chanel No. 5, which was Gran's favourite perfume.

'Right, that's enough.'

Eva felt Gran's hands on her shoulders, making her stand straight.

'Eva, tell me what's wrong. I can try to help if I know what's the matter.'

Eva took a few deep breaths. She felt a bit wobbly on her feet and wished they could sit down, but Gran had taken her elbow and they were walking together down the drive.

'Someone said something,' Eva whispered.

'Hmm,' Gran said. 'It's a common enough occurrence. There's not much I can do to stop that, unfortunately.'

Eva gave a weak smile, despite herself. 'Someone said something about Dad,' she admitted.

'Oh,' Gran said. 'And was what they said true or a lie?'

Eva didn't answer. Jamie had said that Dad was odd, wanting to know where she was all the time. But that wasn't odd. Everyone's parents were like that, weren't they? 'He said . . . he said Dad kept me prisoner.'

Gran gave Eva's shoulder a little squeeze. 'Oh dear. And did you get angry with the person who said that?'

'Yes.'

'And how do you feel about that now?'

'I don't know.'

Gran stopped walking. They were still in the park and Eva could see the great hill in the centre. Someone was right at the top, flying a kite. It soared above the park, whipping away from the person at the end of its taut string.

'Eva. You'll find that lots of people in this world will want what's best for you. But they might not always know what that thing is. Your dad wants what's best for you – he always has. But what happened to Mirabelle has made him very cautious. It sounds like your friend wants what's best for you too. Though they have a very clumsy and rude way of saying it. What matters is, can you love the sentiment even if you don't agree with the expression?'

'Can I do what with what?' Eva asked.

Gran grinned. 'Sorry. I mean can you be pleased that people care, even if you don't agree with the way they show it?'

Eva understood that time.

She wrapped her arms round Gran. 'Mum was lucky to have a mum like you,' she said.

Gran kissed the top of Eva's head.

They walked together in a comfy silence, out of the park and along the road. When they were outside the house, Eva paused. 'I want to say sorry to the person I fought with,' she said.

'Good idea. Will you see them tomorrow?'

Eva looked up at Jamie's house. 'He lives on this street. Can I go over, just for five minutes?'

Gran's neat, dark eyebrows pinched together in a frown. 'You know your dad doesn't like you being out alone.'

'It's just in the street. Just two minutes. I'll be right back. Please, Gran? Pretty please with lipstick on?'

The corner of Gran's mouth twitched. 'Well, OK. But just two minutes. Then I send out the search parties. Which house?'

Eva paused. Gran would change her mind quicker than she could say 'bad influence' if she told her it was the McIntyre house. She pointed vaguely across the street. 'That one. Five minutes. Tops.'

Eva watched until Gran was safely inside the house before dashing up to Jamie's front door. She rang the doorbell. A surge of angry barking skittered towards her from inside the house. A voice yelled at the dogs. But the barking just got louder.

The door opened.

A young man stood holding open the door. One

of Jamie's big brothers. It was like looking at a weird photocopy of Jamie. His brother was taller, bulkier, with shorter hair and a straight-set mouth. But he had the same shape face, the same brown-gold eyes.

'What do you want?' he snapped.

'I'm . . .' Eva wanted to turn and run. The snarling dogs at the man's feet were just as unfriendly as the man.

'Eva!' Jamie yelled from halfway down the stairs. 'Michael, let her in. She's my friend. Wills, Kate, get out of the way, you stupid mutts. This is Eva.'

Michael took a small step backwards, but Eva still had to keep her elbows tucked in so that she didn't touch him as she went past.

The dogs, on the other hand, were all over her. They scrabbled up her legs as though she were a ladder with roast chicken on top. Their mouths were slathery; they were all tongue and teeth.

'Down, Wills!' Jamie said sternly.

The dog ignored him completely.

'Don't mind him,' Jamie said. 'He's as soft as a brush.'

Eva moved through the hall. It was an odd mirror image of her own house, the same shapes, but deco-rated differently. She couldn't help but notice the dog-chewed banisters and the jagged edges where the fake floorboards had come loose. It smelled different too. She could smell laundry, and food, and dogs, and boys. It smelled busy.

Eva suddenly felt shy.

Jamie grinned. 'Shall we go out the back?'

The shed roof. Eva nodded gratefully.

In the kitchen, a woman sat at the table. She had a magazine open and her dark head was bent over a giant crossword.

'Mum,' Jamie said. 'This is Eva.'

The woman looked up and smiled. Eva was shocked to see that one of her front teeth was missing. The woman laughed. 'I take my falsies out at break time. That's how I know it's a break!'

'Don't mind her,' Jamie said, and pulled Eva through the back door.

The dogs followed them outside. Jamie scrambled up on to the roof of the shed. Eva followed. Wills tried to come too, but his legs were too stumpy to make the jump. Kate didn't even try – instead she found a patch of sunlight to flop down in.

'I can't stay long. I just want to say I'm sorry about this morning,' Eva said.

Jamie didn't answer. He lay back on the roof and smiled contentedly. His arms and legs settled out in a star shape. He closed his eyes. Was he going to sleep?

Eva frowned. She'd never been ignored during an apology before. Was he ignoring her? Why invite her in and be nice if he was ignoring her?

He opened one eye slowly. 'You're standing in the sun, you know. You should sit down.'

So he wasn't ignoring her. Eva sat down heavily. The roof was hot underneath her legs. It felt nice. She lay on her back and felt the warmth spread through her shoulders. She felt them relax, almost with a sigh.

'There's no need to say sorry,' Jamie said finally. 'I'm glad you're here now.'

'I can't stay though. My gran is expecting me back.'

'You could stay for tea if you like?'

'No. My dad wouldn't . . . I mean, he says I can't . . .' Eva trailed off, not sure how to tell Jamie that Dad didn't want her to talk to him.

'I know what your dad thinks. He's made that plain. You know, you should tell your dad what you think sometime.'

'I do!'

'Do you? Doesn't look that way from where I'm sitting. Looks a lot like you do whatever he tells you to do, whether you agree or not.'

'You don't understand. He needs me.'

Was this going to be another argument? That hadn't been what she'd wanted at all. Eva took a slow breath and remembered Gran's advice: be pleased people care, even if you don't like how they show it.

Eva looked up at the sky. Stray clouds floated across it, so slowly that she wasn't even sure they were moving. They looked like great cruise ships in a calm sea. 'I wonder what it feels like to be hit by a cloud?'

'Wet and freezing,' Jamie said. 'They might look fluffy, but get close and it's just a huge cold shower.'

She had changed the subject, Eva knew. But Jamie didn't seem to have noticed. He just seemed pleased that they were talking again. Though Dad wouldn't like it, Eva knew. She felt her arms raise in sudden goosebumps as one of the clouds moved in front of the sun. Dad wouldn't like it at all.

CHAPTER 13

'I can walk there by myself,' Eva said the next morning.

'Absolutely not,' Dad said.

She stood by the front door, shoes on, jacket tucked under her arm, emergency coins in her purse. Dad was at the bottom of the stairs, pulling on his trainers.

'Please, Dad. I'm old enough now.'

'No, you're not.'

'Well,' Eva said quietly, 'when will I be? At sixteen? Or eighteen? Or thirty? You have to let me sometime. Why not now? It's broad daylight. The stars are all hidden. Nothing bad is going to happen to me. Dad, you have to trust me sometime.'

'I trust *you*,' Dad said. 'It's the rest of the world I'm not sure about.'

'It's a five-minute walk. I'm not a baby any more.'

Dad paused. Eva could see that there were tears glistening

in his eyes. He nodded slowly. 'OK. OK. I know you're not a baby. But you're still my Bug. If I let you go alone, don't talk to any strangers. Or stop on the way. Promise? And I will call Sally to text me when you get there safely. OK?'

'OK, Dad. And I promise.'

Eva gave Dad a tight hug and then stepped out of the front door alone. She felt a little taller, a little bolder than usual. She smiled at the street lights and grinned at the traffic. The hard tarmac of the pavements felt as soft and springy as clouds. Her feet felt as though they were bouncing her the whole way.

Until she reached the lodge.

Then the smile was wiped clean off her face as though it had never been there.

The driveway looked like a scene from a cop show. Two police cars were parked on the gravel outside. Sally stood next to a police officer. Her face was streaky with tears. None of the children who had turned up to work had gone inside. They stood around the police cars in small huddles. One or two were crying; others looked furious.

Eva felt a cold shiver run down her spine. Was someone ill or injured? She looked around the crowd – there was Shanika and Dilan, together with a few others. Heidi stood alone, looking shocked.

And Jamie?

There was no sign of Jamie.

Eva rushed over to Heidi. 'What's going on? What's happening?'

Heidi turned slowly. Her eyes seemed to have a hard time focusing. 'The lodge has been trashed.'

'What do you mean?'

'Someone came in here last night. Broke in. They've smashed the place up. All the furniture is ruined. There's spray paint all over the walls. Windows broken. It's a mess.'

Eva felt her own eyes prickle with tears. 'Why?' she said finally.

'Who knows? Why would anyone do something like that? They've ruined our work. Who knows whether we can fix it? And, if we do, what's to stop them doing it again?'

Heidi's cheeks were flushed with anger.

Eva looked at the police officers. Another car pulled up and two people with black suitcases climbed out. Their black uniforms had four letters printed on the back. Eva tried hard to make the letters form a word, but she couldn't do it. Her brain felt thick and fuzzy.

'SOCO,' a voice said. Shanika. 'Scene of crime officers. They'll be looking for evidence.'

She'd sneaked up behind Eva and was now staring at her hard. Her brown eyes were full of fury.

'McIntyres. Your friend or his brothers. They'll have been too stupid not to leave evidence behind. Fingerprints, or hair, or something.'

'Jamie?' Eva asked, her voice weak.

'Who else? The McIntyres do stuff like this for fun – everyone knows that.'

'Not Jamie.' Eva was certain of it. He wouldn't do this. He'd worked hard on getting the place done up. He'd painted stars so they could all think about how amazing the world was.

Then she remembered that he'd been made to paint over his stars.

And he wasn't here.

She shook her head. 'It wasn't Jamie. He wouldn't do this.'

Shanika snorted. 'We'll see. The SOCO people will find out soon enough.'

Eva turned to Heidi. 'Can we go in? Can we start clearing up?'

Heidi shook her head. 'No. We won't be allowed in until the police are done.'

Eva looked back at the lodge where Sally stood clutching a tissue. Jamie wouldn't have done this. He couldn't have. Could he?

CHAPTER 14

There was no point hanging around. They wouldn't be allowed in until the police had finished and Sally said that could take hours. Eva wondered if she should go over to Gran's. Dad wouldn't like her being home alone. It's what she *should* do. But Eva knew that she wasn't going to do what she should do. She needed to talk to Jamie. She needed to know that Dad wasn't right about him, that he'd had nothing to do with this. She needed answers.

The street was strangely quiet when she got home. Of course, lots of people would be at work. But there were usually sounds of music, or radios, or playing, even in the middle of the day.

Mostly from Jamie's house, she realised with a wry smile.

Today, his house was silent.

She went and rang the doorbell. She leaned heavily against it and the sound echoed inside the house. Wills and Kate set up a loud barrage of barking.

'Yes?' The door opened a crack and Mrs McIntyre peered over the chain. 'Oh, it's you, love. Listen. This isn't a good time, OK? I'll tell Jamie you called round.'

The door shut again.

Oh.

Eva stood on the doorstep, feeling daft.

Then a window opened and a head leaned out.

'Eva!' Jamie's voice called.

She looked up. His face looked weird from below; his hair fell forward, in an Elvis quiff. 'Eva, I thought it might be you. Well, you or the Feds. Listen, I can't come down right now. Michael and Drew have got stuff they need to talk about. But I'll meet you on the shed in an hour, yeah?'

'What stuff?' she called up.

'Family stuff,' Jamie said. 'They need to get their stories straight. Just in case they need to help the police with their enquiries. I can't talk now, but I'll be out soon, yeah?'

The window closed.

Eva knew what 'getting your story straight' meant. Alibis. They needed to work out what they would tell the police about where they were last night.

And Jamie thought that was OK.

Eva felt sick, cold. She put her hand out against the front door to stop herself swaying. But she hated the sensation of touching that house.

Michael and Drew had trashed the lodge. Jamie had all but said so.

And he was helping his family to hide it.

Heidi was right. Even Shanika was right. Eva had thought she knew Jamie, but she didn't at all. He was a McIntyre through and through.

Eva stepped backwards away from the house. She felt like she was in another bad dream, where the air was too thick to run, too heavy to breathe. She felt as though she would be crushed by the oxygen sinking in her lungs.

She let herself into her own house.

She could tell by the stillness that Dad was still out at work. She'd need to call Gran soon, to tell her that she'd come home early. But she felt strangely tired, as though she didn't have the energy to lift up the phone. Eva fetched a glass of water and stood in the middle of the kitchen.

Jamie was expecting her to meet him on top of the shed.

There was no way she would be there. Dad always said not to talk to strangers and Jamie was a stranger now.

She put the glass, still full, on the worktop.

She crept upstairs, careful not to breathe too deeply. Her chest felt tight as though it was too small for her insides.

This was a feeling she recognised.

She stepped into the spare room at the side of the house. The room that was full of boxes and clutter. The things that Dad had never thrown out, though he had hidden them away. Mum's things.

The spare room looked out over the garden too. She could just see the shed. So she pulled down the blind. Now the room was darker, the sunlight through the fabric was rust-coloured.

A wardrobe stood against the far wall. Eva opened it. There was a gentle waft of perfume from the clothes that hung inside: dresses, jackets, coats, blouses and skirts. A sweet, faint smell that came whenever she opened the wardrobe door. She always worried that one day the smell would be gone, all used up. She crouched down and sat on the wardrobe floor. She pulled the doors closed behind her to stop the smell from escaping.

Now the space was dark, with a seam of light running up the centre of the doors where they didn't quite meet. Once Mum had gone to a 1940s fancy-dress party with her hair set in a victory roll. She had painted her legs with fake tan and asked Eva to draw a line on the back of her calves. Mum said they'd done that during the war to make people believe they could afford stockings. The straight, thin seam of light made Eva think about that now.

When Mum was here, they were always dressing up and putting on plays or dances to make Dad and Gran laugh. Eva had done all the silly voices and Mum had made up the steps. They didn't use scripts, because Mum knew exactly how hard it was for Eva to read and how much it hurt Eva to try and then fail. Instead, they just worked it out. And it always worked out.

Eva reached up and touched the dress above her. She couldn't tell what colour it was, but the fabric was light and summery.

It wasn't fair.

Nothing was fair.

Eva had a horrible broken-inside feeling. As if she were made of glass and something inside her had shattered. She realised that she had tears on her cheeks. She dashed them away.

Eva pulled the dress from its hanger and sat in the dimness, hugging it tight.

Outside, Jamie would be waiting for her on the shed.

He could wait. She wasn't going to join him.

She heard Dad's key in the door.

'Eva?' he called up the stairs. 'Are you home?'

She dropped the dress and spilled out of the wardrobe. He wouldn't like her being in there. It made him sad to remember all Mum's things hidden away in their own room. She moved quickly out of the spare room and on to the landing.

'Hi, I'm here.'

'I heard about the lodge – are you OK?'

His footsteps were heavy as he came upstairs.

'Hey, Ladybug,' he said. 'Come here.' Dad wrapped his arms round her tight. She leaned into him, her arms loose round his neck. The tears came properly now; the sobs shook her shoulders.

'Hush, it's OK,' he whispered. 'It's all OK. What happened was horrible, but it isn't the end. We can fix up the lodge, better than it was before. Hush, Bug.'

His hand patted her shoulder blades.

Eventually, her sobs slowed and became sniffs. How could she tell him that it wasn't the vandalised lodge that was making her cry? She was crying because Jamie didn't care that it had been.

She was crying because she didn't know Jamie at all.

'Come on, let's wash your face and get you something nice and sugary to drink. Hot chocolate? I know it isn't Sunday, but we could have it anyway, as a special treat.'

Eva nodded limply.

Dad helped her to stand. He took her face in his hands and wiped the tear-tracks with his thumbs. 'Right then. Go and wash your face and I'll see you in the kitchen, OK?'

Eva nodded.

She was alone. Before going to the bathroom, she went to her own room. She didn't get too close to the window – she didn't want to be spotted – but she got close enough to peep out.

He was there.

Jamie was waiting on top of the shed, on his back, staring up at the sky.

She felt a twinge in her chest.

How long would he wait? Hoping she'd come? Would he give up and go back to his stinking rotten family? Or would he come and call for her and make her tell him why she hadn't showed up?

She wasn't sure which would be worse.

She went to wash her face.

Tonight she was going to sit, safe and sound with her dad, drinking hot chocolate and watching telly. Things would be just exactly the same as they were before stupid Jamie arrived.

They had to be.

Dad was waiting downstairs. He took in her scrubbed

cheeks and her best attempt at a smile. He dropped a kiss on the top of her head.

'It's horrible when you find out that people can let you down,' he said. 'But it isn't the first time and it won't be the last. I'll always be here for you though – you know that, don't you?'

She did.

And she didn't need anyone else.

CHAPTER 15

'I don't care where he is,' Eva said the next morning.

'Me either,' Heidi said, slipping her arm through Eva's.

'Well, you should care,' Shanika said. 'Jamie should be here to make amends. Everyone else has turned up, ready to get to work. But not him. He hasn't spoken to anyone since this happened. It's obvious whose side he's on.'

Eva thought about saying that she'd spoken to him, but she didn't. After all, they hadn't really spoken – he'd just shouted out of a window and then she hadn't gone to the shed. That didn't count.

She had slept badly and felt tired and grumpy this morning. She was still cross with Jamie, of course she was, but she also kept seeing him laying on the shed, waiting for her, like an abandoned dog waiting for his master. How long did he lay there before giving up?

'Well, there's too much to do here to waste time worrying about him,' Shanika said. 'Has anyone been inside yet?'

Heidi and Eva both shook their heads. Dad had only just dropped Eva off when Shanika and Dilan turned up. There was no way Dad was letting her walk in by herself after what had happened. Other people were arriving in ones and twos. Not just children either. A white van, decorated with pictures of cones and lollies, was backing up the drive.

'Hey, Eva, give me a hand with this,' Brian, the ice-cream-van driver yelled.

She could see that there was something big inside his van, squished up against the fridges.

Brian opened the door and pushed the seat forward. 'It was awkward to get in here, but should be easy to get out if you lot help,' he said.

Eva moved forward. With Heidi and Dilan clambering in beside Brian, and Shanika supervising, they were able to lift it down.

'Our old sofa,' Brian said. 'Nothing wrong with it, really, but the missus wanted one of those where the seat tilts back. We were going to throw this out, but then we heard about the lodge being vandalised. So, now you lot can have it.'

'Publicity,' someone squealed.

Eva threw a stray cushion down from the van and looked to see who had spoken.

'PR!' Shanika said. 'Of course! People were already getting interested, but the vandalism has just made the story hot. Everyone's going to want to know. I wonder if Sally has thought about the angles. We should get in touch with the papers, local news – they'd love this sort of story. We'd get loads of support. Ice-cream-van man –'

'His name is Brian,' Eva interrupted.

'Brian, please wait here while I go and get my phone. This is a perfect photo opportunity.'

Shanika rushed towards the pile of coats and bags that had formed outside the lodge while people waited to see if they could go inside.

By the time she got back with her phone, there was more commotion on the drive. Three men in camouflage gear were trotting up carrying a stepladder and pots of paint. The boot-camp boys. Eva recognised the shouty one, Gary.

'Painting is excellent exercise,' Gary said. 'It really works the triceps. Can we help?'

Shanika clicked away, posing the boot-camp boys on Brian's sofa and sticking Brian up the ladder. 'Say "cheese",' she said.

As more children and parents arrived, the groups in the photos got bigger and bigger until there was no room in the frame for anyone else.

Shanika's face was alight. 'This story is going to be huge,' she said.

It was only when Sally arrived with the front-door keys that the atmosphere got serious again. She pulled down the yellow 'crime scene' tape and unlocked the door.

'Right,' she said, a bit too brightly, as though she was presenting children's telly. 'I'd better see the damage.'

Everyone was quiet as Sally stepped inside. In the silence, Eva could hear Sally's footsteps crunching over broken glass. She was gone for a few seconds, then she reappeared by the door. 'Has everyone got decent shoes on? No flip-flops, or sandals? Just give me a minute to sweep and then I think you can come in, but be careful, OK?'

Shanika put her phone away. As she passed Eva, she stopped. 'You're better off without him. We all are.'

Eva had a feeling that Shan might be right. She followed everyone inside.

The damage was worse than Eva had feared. The chairs had been slashed and their stuffing oozed out like frothing bubble bath. Tins of paint had been poured on the walls and floor, shiny puddles of white and red and black were drying to a tacky finish. Shelves had been pulled down and the objects on them smashed and trampled.

'Why would anyone do this?' Eva whispered. Why would *Jamie's brothers* do this?

She felt Heidi take her hand and squeeze it gently.

Shan righted a fallen chair. 'Because they're scum. That's what my dad says,' she said. 'They see that we've made something good, something to be proud of, and they can't stand it. Because it isn't theirs, they want to ruin it for everyone.'

Eva wondered if she should say something about what she knew, about what Jamie had said. She didn't know for certain that Jamie's brothers had been involved. She didn't have any proof. Other than Jamie looking all het up and saying they'd have to help the police with their enquiries. But maybe that was all it was? Helping the police. Maybe they didn't do it, but knew who had? Could that be it?

Not for the first time, Eva felt queasy with it all.

'But we won't let them win,' Shanika said. There was a brightness in her eyes. They were marble-shiny with tears, Eva realised. 'We're going to make it even better than it was. Starting right now.'

Shan marched to the store cupboard where mops

and buckets and cloths and big bags were stored, and started pulling things out and handing them to anyone who was close by. Eva found herself holding a broom.

Soon the room was full of people tidying and cleaning and moving all the broken things out. She swept up the splinters of wood and balls of couch stuffing, and wondered about trying to stuff the fluff back into the furniture, but the splinters probably meant that was a bad plan.

All around her, people worked. As the pile of debris got bigger, she got sweatier. Someone started singing some pop tune from the radio. Slowly, everyone joined in, until they were shouting the chorus. Eva suddenly realised that she was smiling. She hadn't thought about Jamie or Dad, she'd just been thinking about getting the lodge back in one piece. The same as everyone else. These were her friends: Heidi, Dilan, Sally, even Shanika. Even Shan, she corrected. She might be bossy and rude, but it was only because she cared so much.

If Jamie's brothers were half as nice as Shan, then they would never have done this.

Eva realised that she had made the right choice not to go and see Jamie yesterday. This was where she belonged.

Everyone worked hard that morning. Adults stopped by as the news spread, some brought cleaning equipment, others brought old pieces of furniture that they didn't need any more. One person even brought a computer that he said still worked fine, but he hardly used any more. Another family arrived with a whole box full of sandwiches that they'd made for the workers.

Shan moved through the crowd taking photos on her phone.

'Don't you think the police did that already?' Heidi asked her.

'This isn't for the police – it's for the papers. We've been given an opportunity here. Smile!' Shan held her phone up and Eva heard the shutter-click of a shot being taken. She was pretty sure that she didn't want to be in the paper. She deliberately went cross-eyed for Shan's next shot. Heidi giggled at Shan's outraged look.

When they all stopped to eat, the lodge was looking better already. All the broken objects had been cleared and the worst of the paint had been scrubbed away. The place looked like it had been scoured in the bath and now just needed clean clothes.

Eva chewed the cheese sandwich she'd been given. It was amazing that so many people had come out to help, she thought. But none of Jamie's family was here. Of course they weren't. She looked down at the bread and rolled pieces of the crust into tiny balls.

After break, the rest of the morning passed quickly. The lodge was busier than it had ever been before with well-wishers and workers piling in through the door. More than Sally knew what to do with, really. And Shan continued to click her way through the crowd, taking publicity shots of everyone.

Eva was waiting outside the lodge, ready to go home after a hard morning's work when Heidi slipped her arm through Eva's.

'You live a street over from me, you know. I've seen you walking in sometimes. Do you want to walk home together?' Heidi's blue eyes shone like gemstones.

'I can't,' Eva said. Her answer was automatic. Ever since Mum, she'd said no to invites. It was just easier on Dad. But Heidi's doll face looked crushed.

'My gran is meeting me,' Eva explained. 'She's on her way. But we could all go together? If you don't mind.'

Heidi grinned and her face was sunshine again. 'I don't mind. I love grans. What's yours like?'

'She's nice. You'll like her.'

'It was good today, wasn't it?' Heidi asked. 'It felt like it will be OK?'

Eva nodded. It did.

But that was before she saw what was happening on their street.

CHAPTER 16

Three police cars were parked outside Jamie's house, angled crookedly like toy cars on a rug. Shouts came from inside the building. An officer called out and another reached for her radio. Eva stood stock still. She felt Heidi's grip tighten on her wrist. Gran put a hand on each of their shoulders.

Someone was bundled out of the front door. He had the hood of his jacket up, so she couldn't see who it was. Officers on either side held him by the shoulders.

'It wasn't me. This is an unfair arrest,' the man shouted. Eva recognised his voice – Michael.

Another figure appeared. Mrs McIntyre. Her face was twisted in fury. She spat words as though they were a bad taste in her mouth. 'Let him go. He's done nothing. He was here the whole time. This is discrimination.'

The officers kept walking. They paid her no attention. It was as though she was invisible.

Then Mrs McIntyre grabbed one of the officers and pulled him backwards. Eva gasped. The officer stumbled and fell. In the confusion, Michael wrenched his other arm free and set off down the path. He ran with an awkward sway, like a moored boat on a sudden current.

'Go on, son,' Mrs McIntyre yelled.

Michael leapt over a small wall, heading for the street.

Three more officers appeared from their cars. Michael ran straight into them. They grabbed him tight and dropped him into the back of a police car. His break for freedom had lasted about six seconds and now he was trussed up like a Christmas turkey.

Then Mrs McIntyre was swept into the back of another.

Eva felt sick. Jamie's brother was being arrested.

His mum was being arrested.

Was he here or had they *all* been arrested? Even if Jamie thought Michael was cool, he hadn't had anything to do with the break-in at the club. It wasn't anything to do with Jamie.

She didn't know whether to run towards the house or run away – she wanted to do both at once.

And then another vehicle pulled up. Eva recognised

Melanie sitting behind the wheel of the battered-looking car; it was small and squashed full of file boxes. Melanie got out and strode over to one of the officers. Eva was too far away to hear what they said, but the officer nodded, then spoke into his radio. Melanie went inside the house. She was gone for a few minutes, then she reappeared. She wasn't alone. She guided Jamie in front of her, with one hand on his shoulder. His head was down. He didn't even look up when the police car drove away with his mum in the back.

Eva stepped forward, then broke into a run. 'Jamie! Jamie!' she yelled. But he didn't hear her. Or, if he had heard, he pretended not to.

Jamie fell on to Melanie's passenger seat; the door closed. Melanie got in and the car sped away.

Eva stopped. She was close to her house now. The other cars pulled away too. Only a few officers were left.

'Please!' Eva stepped up to the nearest one. His skin was tanned and crinkled, as if he spent a lot of time outdoors. He smiled at her, though he looked distracted.

'What is it, pet? This is no place to be hanging around. You should get home.'

'Please, he's my friend. The boy in the car. Jamie. Do you know where Melanie's taking him?'

The police officer shrugged. 'No idea, sorry. It's Child Protection's job now. They'll look after him.'

'When will he come home?'

'Here? If they do right by him, they'll never send him back here.'

CHAPTER 17

Eva realised that Gran and Heidi had come to stand beside her. They were the only ones left. The cars had gone; the McIntyres' house was shut up like a keep, silent as a ruin.

'What should we do?' Heidi asked.

Eva didn't know.

'Should we tell Sally and the others? Do you think they were arrested because of the lodge?'

'I don't know.' Eva's mind was whirling. *Poor Jamie*, she thought over and over.

'There's nothing to be done,' Gran said. 'The McIntyres are none of our concern now. You should get on home, Heidi, before your parents start worrying.'

'Mum's not home,' Heidi said cheerfully. 'She won't be for ages.'

Gran frowned. 'Well, maybe you'd better come in with us then. Is that OK, Eva?'

Eva felt suddenly shy. It had been a long time since anyone had come to her house. At school, she was the odd one, the weird one, the one with the dead mum, the one who couldn't read.

Heidi was waiting for an answer. She bit her bottom lip and looked anxious.

Eva suddenly realised that Heidi really wanted to be invited inside. She wanted to be here. It felt like the sunlight got a bit brighter, just for an instant. 'Of course Heidi can come in. I'd like that.'

Heidi grinned and her face went back to its normal, happy expression.

'OK then,' Gran said. 'We all need sugary drinks. That's quite a shock you've both had.'

They followed Gran into the kitchen, and sipped the orange juice she prepared. Then Eva led Heidi out into the garden. There was still a silence from the house next door, but it felt like the kind of silence that followed a shout – just a pause before the next shout came.

Heidi sat on the swing. She pushed herself gently, careful not to spill her drink.

'Where do you think Jamie is?' she asked.

'With Melanie somewhere?' Eva suggested.

'He might have gone into care.'

Eva didn't really know what that meant, not really. She had images of orphanages from films: it was all gruel and rags and angry wardens. And there was Tracy Beaker, of course. She'd seen that on telly. Maybe Jamie was getting up to mischief and hoping that a new family wanted to adopt him.

No.

Eva knew there was no way he'd be hoping that. He loved his family, whatever anyone else thought of them. He'd be wanting to come home.

'He'll be hating it. It's his worst nightmare. He told me that he'd never let Melanie take him away from his family. But he couldn't stop her. This is my fault,' she said quietly.

'How is any of this your fault?' Heidi asked.

'He should have been at the lodge today. If he'd been with us, then Melanie wouldn't have come to take him away. But he stayed home.'

'I'm still waiting for the part where that's your fault.'

Eva felt her face redden. Her cheeks were hot with shame. 'I didn't give him a chance to explain. Last night, he asked me to meet him. But I was angry, so I didn't go. I knew that the police were going to talk to Michael. I'm just like everyone else, judging Jamie by what his family does.'

'Do you think he wanted to explain?' Heidi asked.

Eva nodded. 'He waited for me for ages. He thought I was his friend, but I let him down. If I had met him last night, he might have come to the lodge with us today. He might have helped with the clean-up. He might have been there making it right – instead he was in his house. The police must have called Melanie as soon as they knew he was home. She wouldn't have taken him away if he'd been with us. Oh, Heidi, he thinks that no one cares about him.'

'You care,' Heidi said. 'Sounds like you care a lot.'

'He doesn't know that. And now he's gone.'

Heidi was silent for a moment. She kicked at the scab of dry soil beneath the swing. 'Maybe it's for the best though. Whoever's fault it is. Maybe Jamie will be better off wherever he is now.'

Eva shook her head. 'No way. He loves his family. Even if they are a bit of a nightmare. He's going to hate wherever it is that Melanie took him.' Her nails dug into her palms. She realised that she was feeling angry, as well as guilty.

'Heidi,' she said, 'I need to find him. I need to see that he's OK. I need to say sorry. Maybe even get him back! What do you think?'

Heidi's eyebrows shot up. 'Get him back? He isn't a computer game you've lent to someone. His social worker has taken him into care. You can't just ask nicely and get him back.'

Eva looked at the rickety fence that divided her garden from Jamie's. Sunlight dappled it with warmth. Even the shed looked more golden than brown. It was all right for her. She was here, with Gran and Heidi, and Dad was on his way home. It was all normal. But everything had changed for Jamie, and it was all because of her.

'I have to go and find out where he is,' she said.

'Go where?'

'Next door. Mr McIntyre might be there. Or Drew. I can ask them where Jamie's gone.'

Heidi stood up. She looked horrified, as though a whole cyberman army had materialised next to the swing. 'You want to ask Mr McIntyre if he knows where Jamie is on the day that his wife and son were arrested and his other son has been whisked away by the council?'

Eva nodded slowly. She *thought* that was what she wanted to do.

'Wow. Well, all I can say is what song do you want played at your funeral?'

CHAPTER 18

Eva glanced from Heidi back to the fence and Jamie's house. She imagined walking up to the front door, ringing the bell and asking a distraught Mr McIntyre if he knew where Jamie was. It would be like finding a hornets' nest and telling the hornets that their queen was ugly. She wouldn't get out of there in one piece.

'You're right,' she said. 'I can't ask Mr McIntyre, not today at least. But the longer we leave it the colder the trail will get.'

'Phew. A wise choice.' Heidi sat back down on the swing. 'And are you absolutely, definitely certain that you want to find him? I mean, you're sure that he isn't better off wherever Melanie has him?'

'I'm sure. Jamie will want to come home. No question.'

'OK. So, what's the plan?'

Eva took a few deep breaths. Heidi thought she could come up with a plan. Heidi trusted her, just like Jamie had. She had to think of something. 'Dogs!' she said.

Heidi looked puzzled. 'Not the answer I was expecting.'

'The dog walkers in the park. They could lend us a bloodhound. It could track Jamie down. They can smell tiny traces of scent in the air.'

Heidi shook her head. 'I don't think there even is a bloodhound at the park – it's all Labradoodles and Yorkshire terriers. And Jamie went in a car. They won't be able to trace him. Hey, I know, we should ask Shan – she's clever. She'll come up with something.'

Shan? She wouldn't help Jamie, not in a million years.

Heidi must have seen the thought displayed on Eva's face. 'I know she won't want to help Jamie, but she might help us. Come on!'

'Won't she have gone home? I don't know where she lives.'

'She'll still be at the lodge. She'll be doing something with the radio. Or something. Can you come back there now?'

'I'll have to ask my gran.'

'OK, come on then.'

Eva followed. She'd do whatever it took to find Jamie.

CHAPTER 19

Gran gave them twenty minutes. Back in time for lunch, she said, before Dad got home.

Eva hoped that was enough time to convince Shan. They raced back to the lodge and found Shan in the main hall, sitting on Brian's old sofa. Heidi explained what had happened to Jamie.

'I suppose you've called his mobile?' Shan asked.

Eva shook her head. 'I don't have his number. He lives just next door. I never thought to ask him for it.'

Shan sighed. 'You really do need help, don't you?'

'Does that mean you will help us?' Heidi asked.

Eva grinned. She hadn't thought that there was an 'us', not really. She'd assumed that Heidi would wander off soon, find someone more interesting to be with. But here she was saying 'us' and it sounded as though she meant it.

Shan pursed her mouth. 'I don't see why I should. It's not as though I'm a founder member of the Jamie McIntyre fan club. In fact, I don't like him. He's trouble.'

Eva caught at her lip with her teeth. 'I know what you mean,' she said quietly. 'But doesn't that mean he needs our help even more? I mean, what's the point of helping someone with no problems?'

The door opened and Dilan tumbled in. He was carrying a big net full of footballs. 'Look!' he said. 'Some bloke from the sports shop dropped these off. He heard about the damage and wanted to help. He said he was moved to be generous. Wait till your campaign really gets going, Shan. We'll get loads of cool stuff.' He dropped the net. Twenty or so balls bounced with a weird tinny sound. 'Why does everyone look so serious?' he asked.

'We were just talking about being generous,' Heidi said. 'About whether you should help out, if you can, when someone needs you to.'

'Oh,' Dilan said. He edged a ball with the outside of his shoe. It clattered against the others. 'Well, of course you should. Who says you shouldn't?'

Shan sighed dramatically. 'Fine. Fine, I'll help. And so will Dilan. But don't be surprised if it ends badly, OK? And, if I help you, you need to help me back.

Sally and I have been talking to the local radio station. They want to come down here to broadcast tomorrow. I'll need people here bright and early to help them set up. By "people", I mean you two. Deal?'

'It's a deal. Thank you!' Eva suddenly felt that this might not be impossible after all, that it might be easy to find Jamie. With help from the others. 'Where should we start?' she asked.

'There's no point Googling him. There will be thousands of Jamie McIntyres in the world and he's never done anything that means he'd be on the internet. Unless they list court appearances,' Shan said. 'There is one place, though, where we might be able to find his number.'

'Where?'

'Sally's office. We all had to fill out forms, remember? With our contact details. In case of emergency. His mobile number might be on that. And, luckily, his good-for-nothing brothers made such a mess of the office that Sally won't notice a bit more rifling.'

Eva remembered the form. She had no idea what it said on it, because Dad had filled it all in for her. Forms were like A4-sized panic attacks as far as she was concerned. But Shan was right – the form must have everyone's phone numbers on in case someone got hurt in a random painting accident. If Jamie had filled his in properly, then this would be easy-peasy. Jamie would be found.

'Dil, you go and distract Sally,' Shan said. 'Heidi, keep a lookout. Eva, you're with me.'

'Why do you get to be the boss?' Dilan moaned. 'And who are we helping anyway?'

Shan raised an eyebrow. 'I'm the boss because these two came to me for help. And I'm *always* the boss of you. Off you go. Ask Sally for a game of football or something. Let her win so she doesn't abandon the game. We need at least fifteen minutes to have a good look. The office is in a right state.'

Eva followed Shan and Dilan out of the lounge and into the hallway. Stray bags were starting to pile up there: black bin bags with cushions and curtains in, plastic bags with art supplies, cardboard boxes with board games. Even a PS3.

'Has all this just come in now?' Shan asked Dilan.

'Yeah. Word's got out. The whole town is sending us stuff. We'll have enough for three lodges if it carries on like this.'

'Especially after we're on the radio,' Shan said. 'Now go and find Sally and keep her busy.'

Dilan knocked on the office door. There was no answer. He tried again, a bit louder. Nothing.

'Right,' he said, 'the office is empty. You go in and

be quick. I'll find Sally and keep her distracted for as long as I can.' He ran off down the hall, clutching a football with a hopeful expression.

'Eva!' Heidi called from the main hall behind them. Eva turned, smiling.

'Here.' Heidi held out a piece of paper. 'My phone number. I was thinking, you don't have my number and I'm your friend too. Not just Jamie. You should have my number.' Heidi's face flushed pink as a strawberry milkshake.

Eva took the piece of paper. 'Thank you,' she said.

'OK, if you two can tear yourselves apart for one minute,' Shan said, 'we've got work to do. Heidi, keep an eye out for Sally. Eva, come with me.'

Shan turned the handle to the office door and stepped in slowly. She held up her hand to Eva – *Wait!* Then waved her in when she was sure the coast was clear.

The office was in a terrible mess. It was as though the people who broke in wanted to do the most damage here. It was as though *Michael* wanted to do the most damage here, Eva corrected. The desk was still in one piece, but the wooden chair had been smashed to kindling over it. Drawers had been pulled out and paper lay everywhere like an explosion in a library. It was awful.

'What animals,' Shan said in a shocked voice. 'I hope the police lock up the McIntyre boys and throw away the key.'

'You said you'd help,' Eva said.

Shan's face looked cross. 'I know, we've got a deal. But just because I help you doesn't mean I have to like it. We haven't got long. Jamie's record must be in here somewhere – get looking.' Shan started poking through the drifts of paper, flicking glances at each one.

Eva felt her mouth go dry. She stood still, she was all heartbeat and sweat.

'What? Move!'

'I can't,' Eva whispered. 'I can't read.'

Shanika stood up slowly. She let the pile of papers in her hand drop back to the floor. She turned to face Eva.

Eva felt her cheeks burn.

'Really?'

'Well, I can, but not very well. It takes a long time. The words look like spaghetti unless I concentrate really hard.'

'So concentrate.'

Shan picked up more papers and sorted through them deftly.

Eva bent down and picked up the nearest sheet. The words were held there for a moment, their shapes clear, then, like water dropped on to an ink blot, they seeped into each other and the sense was lost. Eva forced down the panic that was rising inside her.

Shan looked over and sighed. 'You know what a "J" looks like, right?'

Eva nodded. 'J' was a friendly letter; it didn't twist itself round to be different things like 'd' and 'b' and 'p' which were the worst of all.

'Good. Then find anything with a "J" for Jamie at the top and pass it to me. And, next time we break into someone's office to read files, you might want to mention this kind of thing in advance, yeah?'

Eva nodded.

She dropped to the floor beside Shan and picked up a random sheet.

Her eyes skipped over the top – it was a logo and it was bound to be something like the project's name or the council.

'Don't bother with that one,' Shan said. 'We all filled out our forms by hand, remember? So you need a handwritten form with a "J" near the top.'

The pile of scanned pages next to Shan was piling up. Beep, beep, beep. A hundred items logged in seconds. Eva felt the familiar sense of frustration building.

She took a deep breath. And looked again at the next sheet.

The black type gave way to blue ink. Handwriting.

The first blue word began with an 'S'. Not this one then. She dropped it and picked up the next. There was no handwriting at all on this one, it was nothing but typed blocks, like the bricks in a wall laid solid. No good. Next.

Eva flicked through the papers. Not as quickly as Shan, but she was sure she would spot what they were looking for when it appeared. She just had to trust.

'Here!' Shan yelped. She waved a sheet under Eva's nose. 'Got it!'

Eva smiled. That was good, she told herself. It was good they had it, even if it hadn't been her who'd found it.

'We'll get that waste-of-space boy back any minute!' Shan said. Her eyes ran down the page. Her smile drooped like hot lettuce. 'Oh.'

'What?'

'His mobile isn't there. In fact, none of his details are. It's all Melanie.'

'The social worker?'

'No, Melanie the juggling clown. *Of course* Melanie the social worker. It's got her down as an emergency contact.'

'Has it got her phone number? And address?'

'The address is just the council office. Not that she's there much. I think she mostly works out of her car.

Have you seen the state of her back seat? It's like this but worse.' Shan waved at the papers on the floor.

'Shan! What about a phone number then?'

'Oh. Yes. Yes, it has her mobile number.'

Eva's mind was whirring now. They hadn't found Jamie, but they had found someone who knew where he was.

'Write it down,' she told Shan. 'We can ask her where he is.'

'She won't tell you; she wouldn't be allowed.'

'Maybe. But it's the best lead I've got. Write it down.'

'Fine,' Shan said, reaching for a pencil. 'But it won't do any good. Jamie's gone and we won't be able to find him.'

'Yes, we will,' Eva said. 'I know we will.'

CHAPTER 20

Eva sat next to Heidi on the sofa. She turned Melanie's phone number over and over in her hands. Shan stood near the window, pretending that she wasn't really interested.

'Shall I ring her?' Eva said.

'Well,' Heidi said, 'it's a phone number. Seems rude not to ring it.'

'But what should I say?' Eva couldn't imagine any conversation where Melanie would just hand over Jamie's address.

'Start with "hello" and work your way up to "tell me what you've done with my friend or the bunny gets it".'

Eva grinned. Heidi was funny, but not that helpful. 'Shan, what do you think?'

Shan turned away from the window. Her brown eyes

were thoughtful. 'Here's the situation as I see it. There's no way that Melanie would tell *you* where Jamie is. It's unethical, and Melanie wouldn't be unethical. So, what you have to do is to not be you.'

Eva frowned. What exactly was Shan suggesting?

'Can you try that again, but this time in English?' Heidi asked.

'Don't be you on the phone – be someone she *would* tell his address to.'

'Like his mum?' Heidi asked.

Shan flashed her a look that would have withered spring grass. 'No, seeing as his mum is in a police cell. I'd say very much *not* his mum.'

'How about a police officer?' Eva asked.

Shan raised an eyebrow. 'Now you're talking.'

'You can get in trouble for impersonating a police officer. I saw it on telly,' Heidi said doubtfully.

'Then be a community support officer, or a traffic warden, or a coastguard – I don't care. Just try and sound like someone official!'

Eva took a breath and shook her arms. She remembered that she had done just this sort of thing with Mum. She could put on silly voices and act. And Dad was always saying she had a good imagination. She just needed to be convincing.

'Dial the number,' she told Heidi.

Heidi took her phone from her bag and took the number from Eva. She dialled and handed the phone over. It was pink and decorated with sparkly stickers. Eva pretended that it was black, businesslike and attached to a receiver on an office desk. The lodge seemed to disappear around her. She meant business.

'Hello, Melanie Tyndall speaking.'

'Hello, Miss Tyndall. This is Edie . . . er . . .' Her eyes flashed around the room wildly. 'Lodge. Edie Lodge. I was at the scene earlier, where you collected Jamie McIntyre.'

'Oh, are you CID?' Melanie's voice was crisp and direct.

'Something like that.'

'How can I help?'

'Well, we just need to ask some follow-up questions. So I need Jamie's address.'

'Don't you have it? I sent it with my report to the Friar's Brook station.'

'Er, no. Maybe it got lost.'

'Which division did you say you were with?' Melanie asked sharply.

'ICT. I mean, TCP.'

'Who is this?'

Rumbled.

Eva looked at the phone in horror.

Heidi grabbed the phone from her hands and mashed the 'end call' button with her thumb.

The phone immediately began to ring.

'Eek! Melanie!' Heidi held out her phone as if it were a hissing cockroach.

Shan took the phone and pressed answer. 'Hello? No, you must have the wrong number. This isn't Edie. I don't know any Edie. I don't know what you're talking about. I didn't call you. You called me. I didn't –' Shan looked up. 'She hung up on me. That's not very nice. So, did you get an address?'

Eva shook her head.

'Nothing?' Shan asked again.

'No. She said I should get the details from Friar's Brook police station. She took her report there.'

'Friar's Brook?' Heidi sat up straight. 'That's the other side of town. Why would she send his details there?'

Eva nodded slowly. 'You're right. Friar's Brook is miles away, nowhere near our house, or Melanie's office. Friar's Brook must be the station closest to Jamie's new home. Melanie must have taken him there. But where exactly though? Friar's Brook is huge. We can't go knocking on every door looking for him. It would take years. And, now we've made Melanie suspicious, there's no telling whether he'll stay there.'

'Oh well,' Heidi said, 'you did your best. Jamie would understand.'

That was a phrase Eva had heard lots of times – you did your best. Dad said it to her after tests. Mum used to say it to her after parents' evenings. You did your best.

But she hadn't, not yet. If Heidi thought that making one call was her best effort at getting Jamie back, then she had a lot to learn.

Eva hadn't even got started yet.

CHAPTER 21

'The outlook for tomorrow is sunshine with scattered clouds. You're listening to Burn107FM. Here's a tune to get your toes tapping.'

The radio played a bright pop tune that Eva hummed along to. Dad sat across from her at the kitchen table. He dunked a piece of chicken in his sweet chilli sauce.

'You seem a bit better today,' he said. 'Is the lodge recovering?'

'The lodge? Yes. Loads of people came to help today. It's probably going to be on the news tomorrow, Shan says. She's good at P-something.'

'PR? Public relations?' Dad asked with a grin.

'Yes, that's what she called it. I think it means getting people to take notice of you. It's working though. Brian brought a sofa and Gary has loads of sports stuff we can have. And the radio people are coming too. It's

131

nice, isn't it, the way people have helped out? I think people are nice, really.'

Dad chewed slowly. He didn't answer straight away. Then he swallowed and said, 'I think most people want to be good, but they don't always manage it. It's not always easy to know what the right thing is.'

Was he thinking about the McIntyres? Or someone else? Eva didn't know what to say, so she didn't answer.

'We all get it wrong sometimes,' Dad said.

'Not you though,' Eva answered.

Dad gave a sad laugh. 'Even me.'

'You've never done anything wrong.' Eva felt herself getting cross. No one was allowed to criticise her dad, not even him.

'Your gran might not agree. Jaclyn has very strong opinions about the things I'm doing wrong.'

Eva pushed aside the last pieces of chicken. She didn't feel hungry any more.

'I'm sorry,' Dad said. 'I didn't mean to make you feel blue. It's great that so many people have turned up to help you all. Maybe I could come by and get busy with some DIY myself one of these days?'

He took her plate and put the leftovers in the fridge. As he ran the hot tap into the sink, he joined in with the song on the radio.

'Step on it, move on it, jump on it, go, gotta love it.'

Eva laughed as he added dancing moves.

'*Step on it!*' Stomp!

'*Move on it!*' Twist!

'*Jump on it!*' Up!

'*Go! Gotta love it!*' Dad shimmied with a tea towel. 'Come on – dancing is the best exercise.'

Eva leapt up to join in. She stretched and bounced and wiggled and bent.

As she was midway through a hand-jive, she froze.

'Eva? Are you OK?'

She felt a sherbet fizz tingle through her whole body. OK? She was brilliant! She had just thought of a way to get Jamie's new address.

CHAPTER 22

The next morning, Eva opened the fridge. There was a cardboard bucket with the remains of last night's fried chicken in it. No bones. Perfect. She took it out and tucked it under her arm. It was just what she needed for her plan to work.

She had gone through the details on the phone with Heidi last night. Heidi'd promised to get Shan to do her part too.

Dad was still asleep upstairs. But he'd be awake soon.

Eva scribbled a note on the back of an envelope. It took all her concentration to write an explanation. And she was pretty sure that all of her concentration wasn't enough. Even to her own eyes, the words looked twisted and ugly. It might be better to wake Dad and tell him where she was going. But he would stop her immediately, so that wouldn't work. She propped the note up against the toaster.

Outside, Heidi was staring at next door, as though she were looking at an alien spaceship – her eyes saucer-wide as she waited for the inhabitants to appear. Not that they would at this time of day.

Shan was with her, looking cross. 'This better not take long. The radio station is arriving at the lodge in half an hour to set up for their broadcast.'

'It won't take long,' Eva said.

'I really don't know why I'm doing this for you,' Shan said. 'It completely goes against what I stand for.'

'What do you stand for?' Heidi asked.

'Doing the right thing, being responsible, you know, being good.'

'We're doing exactly that,' Eva said. 'Doing the right thing for Jamie. I'm sure of it.'

'So does that mean you've told your dad then?' Shan asked.

Eva felt heat rise in her face. 'I've left a note.'

'That will be a bit late, considering what you're planning,' Shan said. She sniffed. 'Well, if we get caught, I'm telling them that it was all your idea. Is that clear?'

Eva nodded. That was fair enough. It *was* all her idea. She couldn't quite believe that Heidi and Shan were even thinking about doing this, just because she'd asked them.

'Right,' she said. 'Let's do this.'

Eva led her team of conspirators. She had left her invisibility shield at home, but she had brought super speed, super stealth and super friends. Shan was Brains and Skill. Heidi was Bravery and Strength. And Eva? She stomped towards the park, her arms swinging, her head up, her focus keen. She was Bold and Staunch. They were a team and they were going to get Jamie back.

Together they flew along the street, swept through the west gate and raced towards the main gate. Nothing was going to stop them. Not even the little yappy dogs on their morning walks.

'Get down!' Shan snapped as a Yorkshire terrier leapt for her ankle.

'Halt!' Eva shouted.

Shan and Heidi slowed. 'Halt?' Shan asked. 'Really?'

'Have you never watched a spy film? Yes. Halt! This is a good place to prepare.'

They were near the main entrance. The lodge and playing fields were behind them. In front was the road and the few parking spaces that flanked the gates. A blue car with a logo showing skipping ropes and weights on the side was parked there already. Gary's car. A wooden park bench was set immediately inside the gate for those who found the walk from their car too much for them.

Heidi sat down. The others joined her. As she sat, Eva noticed a small brass plaque on the back of the bench. She couldn't read the whole thing – it was small and scratched and the words were too close together – but she mouthed the first few sounds: '*In memory*'. She smiled a tight smile. It was a sign.

'Hey, look! Here she comes,' Heidi said. They immediately moved to their positions.

Heidi took the bucket of leftover chicken dippers and went to lean against the gatepost where she could see the road.

Eva ran and hid behind Gary's car.

Shan stood in front of an empty parking space.

Melanie's car eased into the open bay.

Shan simpered her best simpery smile.

'Melanie!' Shan squealed as the car door opened.

'Shanika, oh hello. I just . . . can you . . . one second.' Melanie was trying to hang up a speaker-phone, pull off her heels and keep the dog in the back-seat, all with one hand.

'Bandit, down! Stay!' Melanie tugged on one trainer. Bandit was a Border collie with black and white mark-ings on his flank and a black stripe across his white muzzle, as though he were wearing a bandit's mask. He hurled himself up and down in the back seat, whimpering with excitement. He strained at the lead that Melanie was trying to hold.

'I wondered if I could talk to you about work experience?' Shan said. 'I know I'm a bit young, but I'd love to know more about what you do.'

'Now? Well . . . erm . . . Here, hold this.' Melanie shoved a jacket towards Shan.

The whining in the back seat turned into a volley of barks. Eva crept round Gary's car so that she had a better view. The barking got louder and reached a crescendo that forced her to cover her ears.

'Bandit, down! Bad boy.'

'I'd come to your office and make tea –'

'Bandit! Stay!'

'I can work a photocopier and a fax machine –'

'No, sit! Wait!'

'I'm good at typing too –'

'Bandit!'

At the gates, Heidi tipped up the bucket. One piece of fried, golden chicken breast fell from the greasy container. It twisted in the air and landed on the ground with a poof of scent. The sudden burst of chickeny goodness was too much for Bandit. He bounded from the car and leapt towards the chicken.

It was gone in one chomping mouthful. Heidi tilted the bucket towards him, so that he could sniff that there was more, and then she turned and ran into the park.

'Bandit! Stay!' Melanie yelled at the escaping dog. 'Come here!'

Melanie ran after the Bandit.

Shan ran after Melanie.

Eva raced from her hiding place. This was her moment!

Melanie had left the car door open. Eva reached in and pushed a scrunch of newspaper and some empty chocolate wrappers off the passenger seat. There was a briefcase underneath all the mess. Bingo.

Her heart pounded like footfalls on a pavement.

Jamie was in here. Somewhere.

She clicked open the clasps.

Paper bulged out of the sides and flipped up in the breeze. Tons of paper, notes, squiggles, words . . . a great, steaming mess of them.

She gulped.

Why had she not held the chicken and got Heidi to do the reading?

Because Heidi didn't want to go to prison on account of Jamie.

It was down to her.

She had to read everything quickly and replace the briefcase.

Or take the whole thing and get one of the others to read it.

It was no choice at all really. There was no way she could read through all the notes in the time it took Melanie to remember that she'd left her car unlocked.

The briefcase was coming with her.

She grabbed it and slammed the car door closed.

'Hey!'

She turned to look behind her, the direction that the shout had come from. A woman in sports clothes was trotting towards her.

'Hey, what are you doing in Melanie's car?'

'It's OK,' Eva shouted. 'She knows me. She asked me to fetch something for her.'

'Really? What?'

The woman was close now. Eva was sure that her pounding heart must be loud enough for the woman to hear.

'Just some notes she wanted to read before the class started.'

The woman frowned. 'Mel never reads in the morning. She's no good for anything before breakfast.' The woman held up two muffins. 'Who are you, exactly?'

Eva had nothing to say. Her mind went blank.

But her body knew what to do.

She clutched the briefcase to her chest, turned and ran into the park.

'Wait! Stop! Thief!' the woman behind her shouted.

Eva picked up the pace, the briefcase by her side banged against her knees, but she tried to ignore the pain. Getting to Jamie was the only thing that mattered now.

That, and not getting caught.

And Dad not finding out.

And not getting Heidi and Shan arrested.

She put on an extra burst of speed. She wasn't sure where she was heading, but she needed to catch up with the others and have one of them look through the files.

Heidi and Bandit were miles ahead, darting towards the hill at the top of the park. Melanie was halfway across the playing field. Shan struggled on behind, but was getting tired. Well, she was Brains and Skill – it was Heidi who was Bravery and Strength after all.

There was a group of people already on the playing fields. They were stretching and bending and jogging on the spot. Gary's Boot Camp.

The woman chasing Eva yelled as loud as she could and the exercisers looked up like gazelles sniffing for lions.

Boot camp ahead and jogger behind: Eva was trapped in a Lycra sandwich.

If only she could leapfrog over the class. One huge superhero bound would take her sailing up over their heads and down right next to Heidi.

Eva couldn't go forward and she couldn't go backward – if she did, she'd be caught. Instead she turned left, towards the west gate. Shan had stopped running too. She looked back and changed direction, trotting to intercept Eva at the play park.

Eva put her head down and dashed through, slinking left and darting right to get away from the confused-looking adults.

Bandit's barking came from far away now, right up on the top of the hill.

'Eva!' Over to her right, Shan stood waving. She had taken cover behind Brian's ice-cream van and was trying to keep out of sight.

Suddenly Eva was hit by a glorious, shining burst of inspiration.

'Brian!' she yelled. 'Brian, start the engine!'

Shan understood in an instant. She banged on the window and yelled Brian's name. The ice-cream seller appeared behind the serving hatch. He took one look at the mob of adults haring after Eva and disappeared again. The next thing she heard was the revving of the engine and 'Greensleeves' tinkling out of the speaker. Shan wrenched open the passenger door, tumbled inside and held the door open for Eva.

Eva was just metres away from the van, but the class of fit, angry adults was right behind.

She hurled the briefcase on to the seat beside Shan and then heaved herself into the vehicle. 'Go!' she cried.

Brian's eyes were practically springing out of his face. 'What's going on? It's not a zombie apocalypse, is it?'

'Drive!' Shan said. 'Please,' she added quickly.

Brian harrumphed, then put the van into gear and they moved forward.

In the wing mirror, Eva could see that the class hadn't given up. There were about twenty of them, running like hounds after a hare. Hounds in tracksuits. And hares in an ice-cream van.

Then she saw a dog with them – Bandit! His tongue lolled out of the side of his mouth as though he were grinning. Was Melanie with him?

'Where am I going?' Brian asked. They were past the play park now and were heading back to the main gate. 'And why are those grown-ups chasing you?'

'We have something of theirs and they want it back,' Eva said.

Brian glanced over, his face crumpled with a frown. 'Something of theirs? You stole something?'

Shan, sitting in the middle of the seat, crossed her arms. 'Brian,' she said, 'we're just borrowing it. We'll give it back. But right now, if you stop driving, then it will all be for nothing. We haven't hurt anyone. We're on a rescue mission. So, if you help us, I promise you won't regret it. I'll even get you a slot on the radio later today to talk about it. Free publicity.'

Eva smiled, sweet as the ice creams around her.

'You can get me on the radio?' Brian asked suspiciously.

'She can,' Eva said firmly. 'She's meeting them this morning.'

Shan glanced at her watch and gasped. 'The radio crew will be at the lodge in ten minutes. I have to get out and get up there.'

Brian had eased his foot off the pedal and the van slowed up. The adults in the wing mirror loomed larger.

'No!' Eva shouted. 'Please, Shan, I need you to read the papers for me. There isn't time to stop. We'll get back to the lodge soon. Anyway, if you get out now, Melanie will whisk you straight into Sally's office for a telling off and you won't get to speak to the radio crew.'

'Would I lose my slot on the show?' Brian asked.

'Yes,' Eva said.

'Well, in that case, why don't you tell me where I

need to go and as soon as you're done I'll take you back to the lodge myself?' Brian slammed his foot back on the accelerator and the van reached its cruising speed of about fifteen miles an hour.

'Friar's Brook,' Eva replied. 'Jamie is somewhere in Friar's Brook.'

'Oh, really?' Brian asked. He sounded worried. 'Only, that's not my patch. That belongs to Ginelli's Fresh Italian Ice Cream. They'll go mental if they see me on their streets.'

The main gate was close now. Brian pressed a remote control and the bollard sank into the ground. The van pulled out between the stone gate posts and on to the road.

Eva gave another glance at the rear-view mirror.

Bandit bounded ahead of the group, barking and leaping into the air.

Behind him, the runners kept pace. An air of steely determination had come over them now. They were going to catch the van no matter what. Sports types could be competitive like that, Eva thought.

And leading the pack – she must have sprinted like an Olympic athlete – was Melanie.

And she didn't look like she was going to give up the chase any time soon.

'We'll keep you safe from Ginelli's and we'll get back

in time for the radio,' Eva said. She sounded certain, but inside she was quaking – she might just be getting everyone into the most trouble they'd ever been in. She just hoped she could keep her promises.

CHAPTER 23

'We need an address,' Eva said, turning her head away from the mirror. 'Come on.'

She pushed Shan into the back of the van and then scrambled after her, still holding the briefcase. They were boxed in by freezers and the ice-cream machine. Shelves ran up one side, crammed with cones, wafers, pots and tubs. The whole placed smelled of sugar and cream. Eva's mouth watered. But this was no time for snacking.

They had to find out where Melanie had sent Jamie.

'Here.' Eva thrust the briefcase towards Shan.

'What's that?' Shan paused. She looked at the small, black case in Eva's hands as though it were a dangerous beast baring fangs. 'This isn't Mel's, is it? You weren't supposed to take the whole thing! That wasn't the plan. You were supposed to find Jamie's file and bring that.'

'There wasn't time. I only had a second and then all the boot campers were after me. So I just took it all.'

She laid the briefcase down on the floor. As Brian turned a corner, it slid towards Shan, like a card being dealt.

'This is bad,' Shan said. 'Really bad. Social workers work for the government, you know. There could be official secrets in there, or anything. We could go to prison for reading classified documents.'

'They can't send me to prison for that,' Eva said. 'I can't read!' For some reason she was feeling ridiculously happy. This was insane, but it was exciting too. Was this how Mum felt when she looked at the ice-white slopes and decided to ski? Eva had never felt more alive. Despite the fact that Jamie was still missing, Shan was furious with her and – she stood and looked out of the serving hatch – yes, the boot campers were chasing after their runaway ice-cream van.

'*Travel news next,*' a cheerful voice came from the radio, '*then we'll join Andy live from a great little project in Elizabeth Park. It's a tear-jerking story we can all get behind. But first here's Katie with what's happening on our roads . . .*'

'That's us!' Shan shrieked. 'We're the great little

story. We're supposed to be there right now! Brian, turn this van round!'

'No!' Eva said. 'Please? We're so close. Jamie's address is in that briefcase. Just take a look and then I'll get out and Brian can take you back to the park. I'll walk the rest of the way. I promise. Please just look.'

Shan looked as though she were going to argue. Then Eva heard the solid clunk of the briefcase clasps being opened. Papers rustled as Shan searched through them all.

'It's not here,' Shan said a moment later. 'Jamie's file's not here.'

'What? It must be!' Eva joined Shan on the floor. 'It's got to be here.'

'It isn't, I'm telling you! I've looked at the names on every single case file here and Jamie is not one of them.'

Eva could have cried. What now?

She had practically kidnapped Shan, they were being chased by everyone, the radio station needed them at the lodge and it was all for nothing. Jamie's address wasn't even in the case.

They were moving down the high street now and shoppers, buses and cyclists were filling up the road. The van was forced to slow down. Melanie and the boot campers were bound to catch up with them any second. Eva felt her shoulders slump. There was nothing she could do.

The papers were everywhere, pulled higgledy-piggledy from the case as Shan had read the names on each one. There was no point in Eva trying to double-check – the more stressed she got the more the words turned into alphabet snakes, twisting and hissing around the page.

But there was something that caught her eye.

'Hey, look.' She picked up a piece of paper that had hearts doodled on it in red pen. Arrows pierced the hearts and there were a few words scattered across the heart confetti. Words she *could* read: *Gary for Mel*, *Mel for Gary*.

Shan tugged the paper out of her hand and turned it over. '*Mel Sykes*,' she read. The name was repeated over and over again in flowery handwriting.

'That's not Melanie's surname. She's called Tyndall,' Eva said.

'No, it's Gary's. He's called Gary Sykes. I put his name on my list for the radio station. Melanie's been practising what her signature would be if they ever got married. Melanie fancies Gary.'

Eva stood back up again and looked outside.

Melanie led the pack that was chasing them down. She had a determined look on her face, like she was ready to run all day and all night if that's what it took. She was here for a marathon, not a sprint.

Gary ran at her shoulder.

And Gary's group was right behind.

An idea blossomed in Eva's mind.

Shan's mobile rang just at that second. Her face looked nervous as she looked at the screen. 'It's Andy from the radio station,' she said, and accepted the call.

'No time for that. I've got an idea. Brian,' Eva said, leaning into the driver's space, 'can I talk through the speakers? Or is it just "Greensleeves"?'

Brian glanced at her while still keeping one eye on the zebra crossing and the people just ahead. 'Yes, you can. There's a mic there.' He waved towards a black box on the dashboard. 'I never use it. Don't like the sound of my own voice. But I think it still works. Just press down the button on the side.'

Eva took up the mic. It was heavy and square, like a box of matches filled with lead. It was attached by a curly cord to the radio set. She pulled it as far as it would go into the back of the van. She was about to speak when the radio presenter blared again.

'Sorry, folks, looks like Andy at Elizabeth Park isn't quite ready for us. Sounds like something very odd is happening there. So here's a song from 1992 that will put a smile on your face . . .'

151

The van slowed right down, then came to a stop.

'Andy, I can explain,' Shan said into her phone.

Eva leaned out of the serving hatch. In front, an old lady walked slowly across the zebra crossing at a speed that would even embarrass a snail. Behind, Melanie was closing in, her face red and shiny with the effort. Her hair had come loose from its ponytail and sprayed around her face in a sweaty halo.

Shan was babbling into the phone, desperate to keep Andy at the lodge until they got back. 'It's an emergency, I promise. We had to. But as soon as we've found him we'll bring the van back,' she said.

Melanie put on an extra burst of speed, desperate to catch them before the zebra crossing was clear. She pulled away from Gary and the rest of the pack. A sprint now.

Eva pressed the button on the mic. 'Greensleeves' spluttered to a stop and a squeal like mice cheering for their favourite football team came from the speakers above the van. Eva shook the mic and the squealing stopped. But all the faces in the street outside were staring at the van. Most people had their hands up over their ears.

'Melanie Tyndall,' Eva said, her voice coming clearly from the speakers, loud and fierce. 'You took my friend away and I want him back. You have information that we need. And we won't stop until we get it.'

'I might stop,' Shan said. She closed her phone. 'The radio station is furious. They want to know where we are. I couldn't fob them off. They can tell there's a story. They've got a nose for news.'

Eva moved out of the serving hatch and craned her head over Brian's shoulder. The woman was still only halfway across the zebra crossing. Eva could have screamed at her.

'Stop!' Melanie's red face appeared in the serving hatch.

'Go!' Eva yelled at Brian.

'I can't!' he yelled back.

Melanie's hands gripped the Formica counter.

Her body lurched up into the serving hatch.

And with a tumble of trainers, wheezing, trackie bottoms and fury, she landed in a heap inside the van.

For a second, no one moved.

'We've just received an interesting update from Andy. It seems the trouble on the roads that Katie was telling us about may have something to do with the team at Elizabeth Park. Andy, can you tell us more?'

Then everything happened at once.

Melanie dived for her briefcase.

Shan scrambled for her ringing phone.

Brian put his foot on the pedal.

Bandit leapt into the van through the hatch.

And Eva grabbed the piece of paper with Melanie's doodles on it.

'What's going on back there?' Brian yelled. 'Keep that dog away from my waffle cones!'

'It's OK – keep driving!' Eva answered.

'No,' Melanie tried to shout, though the wheezing got in the way a bit. 'No . . . stop this van . . . right now.'

Luckily, Brian couldn't hear a word she said and, with the zebra crossing finally clear, the van trundled along the main road towards the town hall.

Eva pulled the paper closer to her chest. Melanie was bent double, still trying to catch her breath. Her empty briefcase was in her hand. Bandit stood guard on top of the pile of papers. But it was only a matter of moments before she lifted her head and said, very clearly, 'You two are in a world of trouble. What were you thinking?'

'I can't talk now,' Shan told her phone. 'The van just got crazier.'

'I just needed to find Jamie. I thought his new address would be in there,' Eva said simply.

Melanie shook her head. 'I'll be speaking to your parents about this – both of you. Now, we need to turn this van round and get back to the lodge.'

Eva took a deep breath.

There was one final, desperate roll of the dice left. She felt a surge of adrenalin in her chest – the surge you might feel just before skiing down a mountain.

'Not so fast,' she said.

'Ooh,' Shan said. 'I've always wanted to say that.'

Eva held up the sheet of paper she'd been holding – the sheet covered in love hearts and Melanie's fantasy signature. In the other hand, she held up the mic.

Melanie gasped. She glanced out of the back window. The runners following them were beginning to be stretched to their limit, splitting into groups like cyclists approaching a steep climb. But Gary was right at the front of the pack, leading the way. He looked as though he could keep running for hours without getting tired.

'Does Gary know about this?' Eva asked, holding up a page of Melanie's loopy, droopy signatures.

Melanie flushed an even brighter shade of red and her mouth goldfished madly.

'Didn't think so.' Eva held up the mic again and her voice crackled out of the loudspeakers. 'I have an announcement to make on behalf of Melanie Tyndall. She is delighted to tell Gary Sykes that she loves –'

'No!' Melanie yelled, and dived towards the mic. Eva held it up above her head. Bandit barked loudly and Shan grabbed his collar to keep him out of harm's way.

'Everyone, freeze!' Eva yelled.

'I've always wanted to say that too,' Shan said peevishly. Her phone started ringing again.

'Freeze,' Eva said, desperately trying to ignore Shan, 'or Gary will hear all about this.' She waved the paper in the air.

Melanie froze.

Shan answered her phone.

'I'll give this back,' Eva said, 'and I won't tell Gary about it, if . . . *if* you tell us where Jamie is.'

'But I can't,' Melanie said with a wail of anguish. 'It's data protection and child safety and . . . and . . . against the rules!'

'Sometimes,' Eva said, 'rules are there to be broken.' She held the mic to her lips. 'Gary, Melanie would like you to know that if you are looking to get marr–'

'Stop!' Melanie yelled. 'Please don't tell him. Please. I could never go back to boot camp again. I'd be so embarrassed.'

'Then tell us where Jamie is!'

Eva was horrified to realise that there were tears glistening in Mel's eyes. 'I can't do that,' she said sadly. 'I can't.'

The van trundled on. Eva wondered if this were

another *fait accompli*, or whether there was a different French word for when all the ideas have run out.

'But,' Melanie said tentatively, 'if I'd put Jamie's file in my briefcase instead of on the back seat of the car, then you'd have it already. *If* I'd done that.'

'I suppose so,' Eva said cautiously. Where was this going?

'And you only want to find him because he's your friend. You don't want to hurt him or anything?'

Eva nodded. Shan snorted, but Melanie seemed not to hear.

'So, if I wrote it down now, and put it in the briefcase, then, I don't know, got some dust in my eye, just for a second, then I can't help what you see. It would be out of my hands. *C'est la vie*, as it were.'

Eva nodded quickly. Mel grabbed a biro from beside the ice-cream machine and took up a scrap of paper. She scribbled quickly, dropped it in the open case and then clapped her hand over her eyes. 'Oh! Something in my eye. My eyes. Both of them.'

Eva grabbed the paper and looked at the twist of words. Shan leaned in, 'Maple Street. Number 19.'

Mel uncovered her eyes. She looked solemn. Was she regretting helping them already? Eva handed back the doodle. 'Thank you.'

Eva turned to Brian. 'Do you know where Maple Street is?'

He nodded slowly. 'It's right in the heart of Ginelli country. You may have to watch my back. But I can take you there, if you really want me to.'

'I want you to,' Eva said. 'Let's step on it!'

CHAPTER 24

'We go live now to Andy – he has tracked down the two tearaways who have stolen an ice-cream van and kidnapped a social worker and are causing the traffic build-up on the high street. Over to you, Andy.'

Shan looked from her phone to the radio in horror. 'Hello,' she whispered into the receiver.

'*Hello,*' her own voice came, a heartbeat later, from Brian's radio.

Shan was on air!

'*Shanika! This is Andy from Burn107FM. You're speaking live to the county. Can you tell us why you've kidnapped a social worker?*'

Shan's dark eyes were wild with panic. She held the phone between two fingers as though it were a snotty hanky she'd found on Dilan's floor. 'What do I do?' she asked.

'Tell them the truth,' Eva said.

Shan spoke into the phone, trying not to touch it too much. 'It wasn't me who kidnapped anyone. It was Eva. I'm just here to help with the reading.'

'Shan!' Eva couldn't believe what she was hearing. Was that really what Shan thought? 'No one kidnapped anyone.'

She heard her own voice come out of the radio. She was near enough for it to be picked up.

'And where are you taking the social worker? Is this a cry for help, or a mindless act of teenage rebellion? What are your demands?'

'We're not rebelling,' Shan said. 'We're just trying to find Jamie.'

'Is Jamie your gang leader?'

'Just hang up!' Eva said.

'I've got to go now,' Shan said into the phone, and out of the radio.

'Is the social worker OK? Has she been harmed in any way?'

Melanie seemed to snap awake. 'I'm fine!' she yelled, loud enough to be picked up by the radio. 'Honestly!'

Shan hung up the phone. She dropped it down on the floor as though it were burning hot. Bandit sniffed it warily.

'You're listening to Burn107FM. We've just been

160

hearing from the teenage gang who have kidnapped their
social worker and stolen an ice-cream van. Last seen turn-
ing off the high street towards Friar's Brook with crowds
of people in pursuit.'

Eva looked out of the rear window.

There really were crowds following them now.
Shoppers, people pushing prams, dog-walkers, old,
young, tall, short, fat, thin – people of all shapes and
sizes had joined Gary's class and were chasing them,
whooping and cheering as they ran.

'Can't this thing go any faster?' Eva asked Brian.

'No, it's electric. Top speed of fifteen miles an hour,
but very environmentally sound,' he said. 'Don't worry
– we'll be there soon.'

Eva felt wound up tight inside – the crowd behind
them, stealing Melanie's briefcase, the radio station
thinking they were a story – everything seemed to be
pressing in close and twisting inside her. She had to
keep focused on Jamie. Brian would get them there
and it would all be OK.

'Uh-oh,' Brian said.

The van slowed.

'What is it?' Eva scrambled to the front to look over
his shoulder.

'Ginelli's,' he said. 'They must have been listening
to the radio too.'

Parked across the middle of the road was another ice-cream van. It was white, with green and red lettering across the sides. She recognised a capital 'G' at the start of the word.

'Ginelli's?' she whispered.

'It's an ambush.'

The Ginelli's van suddenly started blaring out music – it sounded like the theme tune to Match of the Day.

'Oh no,' Brian said. 'Their battle cry. That'll bring more of them.'

He shoved the van into reverse and checked his wing mirror. The van lurched backwards, gaining speed as it moved.

'Wait! What about Jamie?'

Brian shook his head. 'I'm sorry, pet. But it's just got too dangerous. I can't go any further. You don't know what will happen to a van caught outside its territory. It's waffle-cone carnage. We'll not get out of here in one piece. Blast! Those joggers are blocking the escape.'

Eva looked back. Gary, the class and the growing crowd had turned down the street and were running towards the rear of the van.

In front of them the Ginelli's van was playing its battle music and revving its engine. They were trapped between a rock and a hard place. Or, rather, between Gary and a soft scoop.

'On foot!' Eva yelled. 'Which road is it? I can run there.'

'It's straight up here for a hundred yards. First right on to Nutgrove Terrace, then second left on to Maple Street. It's not far. I'll hold them all off for as long as I can,' Brian said. 'I'll buy you enough time for you to make your getaway.'

'Thanks, Brian,' Eva said. 'I owe you one.'

'Not so fast.' Shan stood up. She grinned. 'I *really* always wanted to say that.'

'What?' Was Shan seriously going to stop her now when they were so close?

'You can't read the street names. I'm coming with you.'

Eva felt her heart swell.

'Woof!' Bandit barked, and tumbled out of the door alongside them.

'I'd better come too,' Melanie said. 'The least I can do is make this a suitably supervised visit.'

From far in the distance, but heading their way, came the sound of another ice-cream van playing the Match of the Day jingle.

'Reinforcements!' Brian shouted. 'Everyone out. Quickly, before they get here.' He looked sad. 'It's been nice knowing you all.'

Melanie paused. She was midway out of the van. 'Is it really that bad?' she asked.

Brian nodded slowly. 'There are strict codes to selling ice cream. I've broken every rule in the book coming into their territory. They'll ruin my van. But it's only fair. I've only got myself to blame.'

Melanie glanced at the girls. Then she looked at Gary and his boot campers who were nearly upon them.

'Well,' Melanie said. 'Looks like the cavalry have got here just in time. Bandit, heel!' She rested a hand on the dog's head. 'We'll stay with Brian. I think I can convince Gary to help here. We'll keep him safe from Ginelli's until the road clears enough for him to pass. You two, go and find your friend.'

'We will,' Eva said solemnly.

'He's not my friend,' Shan added. 'He's Eva's. I'm just going to help read the signs.'

Eva grinned. She wasn't sure that this was entirely true. She had a feeling Shan was starting to enjoy herself. Maybe it was hearing herself on the radio that had done it. Or maybe Shan wasn't as mean as she'd thought. Either way, Shan was becoming a friend too.

'Come on,' Eva said. 'Let's find him.'

She set off at a sprint. Bandit whined and then

decided to stay with his mistress. Shan and Eva were on their own.

'Nutgrove Terrace, then Maple Street,' Shan yelled. 'Here we come!'

CHAPTER 25

Now they ran down tree-lined streets, past redbrick houses set back from the road. Judging from the size of them, Jamie was staying somewhere with at least two bathrooms, Eva thought. An idea flashed through her head . . . Would he even want to come home? She shook it away – of course he would. Home was every-thing to him. He wouldn't swap that for an en suite bathroom and fruit trees in the garden.

On Maple Street the trees were taller and thicker. None of the houses were joined together. Sleek cars were parked on gravel drives outside lots of the houses. Eva and Shan crunched their way up to number 19.

'What if he's not in?' Eva whispered. 'What if he doesn't want to see me?'

Shan rolled her eyes. 'Ring the doorbell before we die of old age.'

Eva did as she was told.

A bell sounded somewhere deep inside the house. It took an age before they heard footsteps approaching. The twisting feeling inside Eva's stomach was getting worse and worse.

Then the door opened and Jamie stood in the hallway.

His face looked surprised, then it flushed red and angry. 'What do you two want?' he said.

'Jamie,' Shan said. 'I see those charm-school classes are really paying off.'

'Jamie, I'm sorry,' Eva blurted out. 'Don't be angry with me.'

'I waited for you.' His eyes looked hurt. 'I thought you were my friend. Not like the others. I waited for you on the roof for hours, but you didn't come. I waited.'

'I know.' Eva didn't know what to say. She had taken the plunge off the mountain, all fizzing with excitement, and now she was at the bottom with all the puff taken out of her.

Jamie began to shut the door.

'Now hold on one minute,' Shan said. She shoved her foot between the door and its frame to stop it closing. 'This girl has been through enough because of you. It's chaos back there. Ice-cream van wars and the radio and the boot campers all fighting. And Melanie taken captive.'

'She wasn't a captive!' Eva said quickly.

'And Bandit jumping through windows and the lodge full of journalists, all looking for a story. All that just for you. The least you can do is listen. And probably say sorry yourself.' Shan took her foot away and stood with her arms folded across her chest.

Jamie didn't answer. He looked like all the breath had been knocked out of him too. He stepped back from the doorway and let them in.

The hallway had shiny tiles set like a chessboard on the floor. A hatstand stood to one side with a pot full of umbrellas rooted beneath it. Further along the hall, framed old maps and line drawings were displayed, winding up a wide staircase.

This house was about three times the size of their homes, Eva thought.

'Are you OK?' she asked quietly.

Jamie shrugged. 'They're nice enough to me here. I've got my own room. It hasn't got a telly in it though. And they want you to take your shoes off inside.'

Eva bent down to take off her dusty trainers. She noticed that Shan had her sandals off already – maybe they had the same rule in her house.

'Who's at the door, Jamie dear?' a voice said from the back of the house.

'A friend of mine,' he shouted. He gave a cross look at Shan. 'And someone else.'

The woman who had spoken appeared from a far room. She had blonde hair done in a scraggly bun and wore loose, cream-coloured clothes. She had a string of amber-coloured beads round her neck.

Eva smiled.

The woman didn't smile back. She looked confused, her eyebrows pinched together.

Shan stepped forward; she had her hand outstretched. 'How do you do? We're friends of Jamie's from his work project. I'm Shanika and this is Eva. We won't be here for long. We just needed to see how he's doing. I hope it isn't an imposition?'

The woman's face relaxed. 'Well, hello, dear. I'm Mrs Grayling. This is a little unusual. In temporary-care situations. But as you're here I suppose it can't hurt. Do you want to take your friends into the drawing room, Jamie?'

'No. The garden,' he said sullenly.

'OK. I'll bring some juice out.'

Eva and Shan followed Jamie through the house. The kitchen was huge, an industrial-sized cooker sparkled spotless at one end and a massive table, shiny and smooth as an ice rink stretched across the other end. There was plenty of space in the centre of the room and the glass doors opened out on to the garden.

It was lovely – like a magazine.

Eva felt her heart clench tight. What if Jamie wanted to stay here? What if he never wanted to come home? What if she'd lost him for good?

Jamie led them away from the trimmed lawn, the blooming flowers, the neat, clean paths. He led them to the side of the house to where an enormous double garage straddled the drive. A garage with a flat roof.

Eva smiled. Maybe it would be OK after all.

Jamie climbed up on to a water butt, stretched up to grab the roof and hoisted himself so that he was looking down on them.

Eva followed.

With a roll of her eyes, Shan climbed up last.

This roof wasn't so different from the one at home. The same speckled rough stuff in patches on the flat surface. It was bigger, that's all. Much bigger. It was about the size of a basketball court.

'Nice place you've got here,' Shan said.

Jamie ignored her. He went and sat on the edge of the roof, overlooking the drive. His legs hung down in the way a different kind of boy might sit on a pier, watching the sea. Eva sat next to him. The gutter pressed into the back of her calves, but it wasn't too uncomfortable. Shan sat too.

'Is Melanie really captive back there?' Jamie waved vaguely in the direction they'd come from.

'Not any more,' Eva answered. 'She was just . . . helping us with our enquiries.'

Jamie smiled despite himself.

'I needed her to tell me where you were.'

'Why?' Jamie asked suspiciously.

Eva looked at him; his gold-flecked eyes looked lost. 'I needed to see you again. I wanted to say sorry. For not meeting you. For not letting you explain.'

'Explain what?'

Eva paused, then said gently, 'You knew, didn't you? You knew that Michael and Drew broke into the lodge.'

'That hasn't been proved! Innocent until proven guilty, that's the law,' Jamie said.

'But they did, didn't they?' Shan asked.

Jamie seemed to crumple. 'I guess so,' he said.

'Why?' That's what Eva found so hard to work out. 'Why did they do it?'

'I told them about the mural, about having to redo it, with Mel watching the whole time and Sally behaving like I was a leper. I think they thought they were sticking up for me. They shouldn't have done it, but they're my brothers.'

Jamie lifted his head and looked straight at Eva. The flecks of gold in his eyes seemed to glisten like embers. 'I'm sorry for what they did,' he said.

'I'm sorry too,' Eva said straight away. 'If I'd met you that day, on the roof, you might have been with me at the lodge when Melanie came for you. You might not have been taken away.'

Jamie shrugged. 'I don't know. It probably would have happened sooner or later anyway. And it isn't for long, Mrs Grayling says. Mum will be home soon.'

'That's good,' Eva said. 'We want you back.'

Shan made a small harrumphing sound.

'Eva!' The shout was faint, but insistent. 'Eva!' Someone was calling her name. Someone hidden by the green lollipop trees that lined the street.

But she recognised the voice.

'Dad?' she said quietly.

'Eva!' Dad's shout was a wail of anguish, as though she were lost at sea and he were walking the cliffs.

She could see him now, a flash of movement along the avenue, blue and white between the green and brown. He was looking for her.

'Dad!' she shouted.

He stopped running, turned in the direction of her voice. Even from this distance, she could see the tightness of his face, the tenseness of his shoulders.

'Dad, over here!' She waved.

In the corner of her eye, she noticed Jamie drawing up his legs and wrapping his arms round his shins.

Dad was on the drive now. Crunching gravel with each quick pace. And Eva could see that he was furious.

CHAPTER 26

Dad looked up at the three of them on the roof above him. His eyes stopped on Jamie. 'You,' he said. 'I should have known.'

'He hasn't done anything,' Eva said.

She could feel the tension in Jamie's body. He was crouched next to her, still and silent, like a dog waiting for a kick.

Dad's eyebrows were furrowed in curtain-folds above his nose. 'Then why have I just heard about you on the radio? Why aren't you at home where you're supposed to be? I wake up, I assume you're upstairs in bed. Then I find a note that I can't make head nor tail of. Then I turn on the radio and all they're talking about is you! Do you have any idea how I felt when I realised you were missing? Do you?' Dad dragged his hands through his hair.

Eva felt her stomach churn. Dad must have been desperate. She hadn't thought of him, not once, since she'd left the house that morning. But she was all he ever thought about – she knew that.

'I should have known that the McIntyre boy was at the bottom of this. He's a bad influence. I told you he was. I told you to stay away from him,' Dad said.

'I know, I'm sorry but –'

'No,' Dad said. 'Get down from there now. You're coming home. I'll call your Gran and she can take you for the rest of the holidays. I should never have listened to her in the first place. You're staying with your family and that's that.'

'But, Dad –'

'No arguments. This is the last time he leads you astray.'

Shan coughed pointedly.

'What?' Dad snapped.

'Well,' Shan said, 'I just think it's important to remember that Jamie has been here all day, with no clue about what's been going on. It was someone else entirely who thought it was a good idea to take files and ice-cream vans and social workers.'

Eva took a deep breath. Shan was right. This was all her doing and if she didn't say so now then she was as bad as Michael and Drew.

175

'Dad, it's true. This was all my idea. Jamie had nothing to do with it. Look, wait there, please.'

She stood up, walked back to the water butt and lowered herself down to the ground. In seconds, she was at the front of the garage.

Now that she wasn't looking down at him any more, she could see how frightened he looked. His skin was pale and sweaty, and his pupils were wide, despite the sunlight.

He had looked like this before. The night he came home from holiday for the last time. The night he had lost everything. Everything but her.

'Dad,' she said gently.

'No,' he said. 'No. I won't have this.'

'Yes,' Eva said, 'I know. But *I* did this, not Jamie. You have said what you thought about Jamie and the lodge and all this, but I never have.'

He looked confused for a second. Then the confusion was wiped away, replaced with the same solid look of certainty that Dad had been wearing like a mask for the last two years.

And Eva knew now that it *was* a mask. The panic and fear were there, just below the surface; they had been since Mum had died. Jamie had seen it too, though she hadn't wanted to believe him.

'Dad,' Eva said gently. 'Mum's gone. But I'm not going anywhere.'

'This has nothing to do with Mirabelle.'

'I think it does. You want to keep me safe. I understand that. But life isn't safe, not always. I think sometimes you have to take risks to feel alive. Otherwise we might as well be dead too. When I woke up this morning, I felt like I was standing at the top of a snowy mountain, with the run below me and the air all clean and crisp. I felt that way because I knew I was going to take a risk. And, Dad, it felt good.'

Eva could see tears in his eyes, his blue irises shining with them. Eva felt her own eyes sting. 'Jamie matters. He's my friend. And I wasn't going to let him go. So I took the risk. And look! Here I am!' She tapped her chest with her palms. 'I'm fine! Nothing bad happened. Dad, Mum's gone. But we're both still here.'

Dad wiped his eyes with the back of his hands. 'Is that how you feel?'

'Yes. Yes it is. We can't be angry with her any more. What happened was an accident.' Eva reached out and took Dad's wet hands in hers. They felt big and rough, they way they always did. But, somehow, it felt like she was the grown-up, trying to make him feel better.

Then his arms were round her and he lifted her into the air. She held him close and could feel him crying as he hugged her back. She closed her eyes. With her head resting on his shoulder, she thought she could smell snow, clean and crisp and far away.

'It isn't fair,' Dad whispered.

'I know.' She wasn't sure if he meant Mum, or Jamie, but she held him tight anyway.

When he put her down, she saw Shan, wiping her own eyes. Next to her Jamie still looked frightened – waiting for a blow to fall.

She smiled through her tears. 'Dad, nothing bad is going to happen to me. You have to give Jamie a chance. Get to know him, then make up your own mind. Please? For me?'

He nodded slowly. 'I think I can do that.'

'Come on then,' she said.

'What, *now*?'

'Of course now.' She led the way to the water butt. Mrs Grayling came out of the French doors with a tray of orange squash.

'Oh,' she said, surprised, 'another visitor.'

Dad's face flushed. He had streaks of tears on his cheeks. Eva could see that he didn't know what to say.

'This is my dad,' she said. 'He's come to give Jamie a chance. Is that OK?'

'Well, if you want to give him a chance, I'd better get another glass.' She handed the tray over and disappeared back towards the huge kitchen.

'Up there?' Dad asked, tilting his head towards the roof.

'Up there,' Eva agreed.

It wasn't easy to get the tray up without spilling any of the squash, but they managed it together.

Jamie and Shan stood up as they walked towards them.

For a second, they all stood in a circle, on the roof, looking at each other.

Then Jamie smiled. 'Did you know that the stars are there, above our heads, even in daylight. They're there right now this second, shining down on us, even though we can't see them? That makes me feel better when I feel sad.'

Dad nodded slowly. 'I guess they are. Yes, I guess they must be.'

CHAPTER 27

'Shall I put this here?' Eva placed the cardboard box she was holding on the pavement.

'Thanks, Ladybug.' Dad shifted the other boxes around in the boot of the car to make room. 'Is that the last of them?'

'There's one more. Heidi's bringing it.'

Eva could feel the heat of the tarmac through her sandals; it was another blue-sky day, but there was a cloud-shadow on Dad's face.

'It's for the best, Dad. It's time.'

'When did you get to be so wise?' He laughed.

It was hurting him to pack up Mum's clothes, to give them away. Eva knew that. It was hurting her too. But she couldn't hide in a wardrobe any more. It was time to say goodbye to that.

'Here you go.' Heidi appeared beside her. She passed

the last box to Dad who put it in the car and closed the boot.

'Thanks for helping,' Eva said to Heidi.

'It's OK.' Heidi slipped an arm through Eva's.

'Do you want to come with me?' Dad asked. 'Shan's given me the address of the charity shop that wants them, but you could help navigate?'

Eva shook her head. 'No, if you don't mind, I'll stay here. Jamie gets home today and we want to take him to the lodge to show him everything now it's finished.'

Dad nodded slowly. 'Yes, but it might be better to wait a day or two. He might prefer to spend his first day back with his mum and dad. They have a lot of catching up to do.'

'Well, we'll wait,' Eva said. 'We'll wait until he's ready. We'll always be here for him, like the stars.'

ABOUT THE AUTHOR

Elen Caldecott graduated with an MA in Writing for Young People from Bath Spa University. Before becoming a writer, she was an archaeologist, a nurse, a theatre usher and a museum security guard. It was while working at the museum that Elen realised there is a way to steal anything if you think about it hard enough. Elen either had to become a master thief, or create some characters to do it for her – and so her debut novel, *How Kirsty Jenkins Stole the Elephant*, was born. It was shortlisted for the Waterstones Children's Prize and was followed by *How Ali Ferguson Saved Houdini* and *Operation Eiffel Tower*. Elen lives in Bristol with her husband, Simon, and their dog.

www.elencaldecott.com

Check out the **Elen Caldecott Children's Author**
page on Facebook